THEDETOUR

THED

ETOUR

S. A. BODEEN

SQUARE
FISH

FEIWEL AND FRIENDS
NEW YORK

**SQUARE
FISH**

An Imprint of Macmillan
175 Fifth Avenue
New York, NY 10010
fiercereads.com

Our books may be purchased in bulk for promotional, educational, or business use.
Please contact your local bookseller or the Macmillan Corporate and Premium
Sales Department at (800) 221-7945 ext. 5442 or by e-mail at
MacmillanSpecialMarkets@macmillan.com.

Library of Congress Cataloging-in-Publication Data
Bodeen, S. A.
The detour / S.A. Bodeen
pages   cm
Summary: Seventeen-year-old Livvy Flynn, a bestselling author
of YA fiction, is kidnapped by a woman and her apparently manic daughter who
have no intention of letting her go.
ISBN 978-1-250-09067-6 (paperback)   ISBN 978-1-250-07863-6 (ebook)
[1. Authors—Fiction.   2. Kidnapping—Fiction.]   I. Title.
PZ7.1.B64De 2015   [Fic]—dc23   2015013378

Originally published in the United States by Feiwel and Friends
First Square Fish Edition: 2016
Book designed by Eileen Savage
Square Fish logo designed by Filomena Tuosto

1   3   5   7   9   10   8   6   4   2

AR: 4.4 / LEXILE: 620L

{ For Lori & Kristi, who know all my secrets }

HOW OFTEN DO you see a girl standing barefoot on a log by the side of the road, playing a flipping flute?

Never, that's how often.

Which is why my focus left the winding gravel for a split second too long, *which* turned out to be way more than enough time to catch the tires of my red Audi convertible on the raised edge of the road, *which* I happened to be driving along much too fast.

I never should have been on that godforsaken stretch of gravel road on that sunny June Friday in the first place. The smart thing would have been to listen to my mom and stay home to finish my novel for the upcoming deadline.

Instead, I had caved in to my pride.

"I'm a real writer, Mom. An *author*, for God's sake. This is what authors do. Authors go to writing retreats." I left out the last part of that sentence, the part that continued on in my head long after my mouth had closed. Authors go to writing retreats . . . *so all the wannabes who pay dearly for the privilege can suck up to us, fantasizing they will be us one day.*

Several of my weekends that summer had been spent communing with the unpublished—oh my bad, *sorry!*—the *pre*-published, the majority of whom are earnest, eager housewives well over thirty who firmly believe that they are meant to be the next Stephenie Meyer.

I had smiled as I stood in my room packing for the weekend retreat, the weekend retreat that I was getting paid a ridiculous amount of money to attend. Because it was funny, really, that the joke was on all those middle-aged moms who didn't stand a chance. They were deluding themselves, thinking they were ever going to make money off their stupid stories and live the dream. The fame, the book tours, the fans. And I loved, *relished* even, that I was seventeen, less than half the age of most of them, and had already accomplished what none of them probably ever would: written a book, a *trilogy* in fact, for which a major publisher in New York City had paid me a whopping mid six figures.

Those people were all fooling themselves.

I mean, seriously, what did they expect from me?

That I was going to recommend them to my agent?

Give them a story idea?

Tell them how to write *the* book that would change their lives?

There was no magic formula. And even if there was, I certainly wasn't going to give it up.

I was seventeen years old. At fifteen, I'd gotten a three-book deal, and at sixteen, I'd gone on a twelve-city tour, chaperoned by my mom and my own publisher-appointed handler.

The first two books of my YA series had been on the *New York Times* bestseller list for thirty-six straight weeks and counting, and between them and my new movie deal—Steven Spielberg himself wanted to take me to dinner when I went to Hollywood in the fall—I was well on my way to having more than a million dollars in the bank. Well, most of it was in a trust for when I was older, but I did get my hands on enough to write a check for the upcoming fall quarter at the University of Oregon, my dad's alma mater, where I would have a single room in the Global Scholars Hall, the most expensive dorm on campus. Pity the poor freshmen on financial aid who would be stuck in rooms barely larger than closets, eating crusted-over macaroni and cheese in the dining hall or boiling Top Ramen in the basements of their dorms, while I would be eating made-to-order sushi.

My success only confirmed my feeling that if those so-called writers hadn't been able to do by thirty what I'd done by sixteen, then they didn't deserve to be published.

In my humble opinion.

My mom had also let me take out enough money to buy a few things, like my bright red Birkin bag, which happened to perfectly match my convertible with Oregon vanity plates that read WRTRGRL: the very same car that lost a bit of stability when I hit the edge of the gravel road while going over sixty when I should have been going closer to thirty.

But it wasn't my fault that I was driving so fast. My unsafe rate of speed was a result of the fact that I was frustrated and very pissed off.

The writing retreat was remote, back in the woods somewhere on the highway between my home in Bend and the city of Eugene, but near the end of the trip I hit a detour. And my car's state-of-the-art GPS kept telling me, in a lovely British accent that sounded almost like J. K. Rowling, to continue straight while my gut screamed that a quick and tidy U-turn was the better option.

So I'd been on the gravel road for about six miles, sun beaming down on my head, J. K.'s "Continue straight" serenading me every now and then, when I finally shouted into the open air, "This sucks! I am seriously turning around."

But then, rounding the next turn, the log came into view.

The log with the girl standing on it.

The girl's long, dark pigtails contrasted with the white of her Hello Kitty T-shirt. There were holes in the knees of her faded jeans. As she balanced, her bare feet molded around the moss-covered log, her neatly bent arms held the flute at perfect attention for a conductor visible only to her.

What struck me most was her expression: Her eyes were dark and narrowed, as if she was angry.

I don't know if it was the sight of that furious flute-playing girl standing on a green log at the edge of the woods, or the fact that my writer's mind immediately began asking questions.

Why is a girl playing the flute on that log?

And why does she look mad?

Whatever the cause, that moment of lost concentration led to the tires catching the side of the road.

Without warning, the world churned.

I screamed.

The blue of the sky and the green of the treetops were juxtaposed in a rush of crunching metal.

The side air bags punched out and kept me from getting crushed. But even as they cushioned my left side, the front air bag didn't deploy. My head smashed against the steering wheel, and all went dark.

I CAME TO WITH A START AND A GASP. I WASN'T SURE HOW MUCH time had gone by. The sun was still high in the sky. My teeth didn't feel fuzzy, so I hadn't been out that long. A few minutes maybe. But everything was different.

I hung upside down, hugged by the seat belt, my white camisole and gray cashmere sweater bunched down around my bust. My position, along with the pervasive smell of gasoline, made the contents of my stomach—a nasty tuna sandwich on sourdough—begin to creep their way up my throat. J. K. Rowling sounded haggard, yet also very determined, as she persistently announced, "Recalculating route. Recalculating route."

It felt as if someone had taken a hammer to my head.

I started to raise my left hand but cried out at the pain in my shoulder and realized I had better move more slowly. Or maybe not move at all.

I blinked a few times. The light hurt my eyes, so I kept them shut.

"Recalculating route."

5

"Shut up." I wiggled my toes and kept going, twirling my ankles, bending knees. Everything seemed okay except for my left shoulder and my head. Once I got out of that car, I was going to be fine. A little banged up maybe, but I could probably use the experience as inspiration for another book eventually. Or maybe, if I milked the drama, it could get covered as a news story—KGW in Portland, then maybe even the *Today* show? How many books would sympathy sell?

As soon as I was upright, I would get my publicist on it.

And then I heard something besides J. K. and the ticking of the engine and the beating of my own heart.

The sound was not coming from my car.

The tone was too steady. High-pitched. Fluttering.

A soundtrack to a documentary about fairies and small woodland creatures.

Was that a—

Despite the pain in my head, I opened my eyes, wincing as I blinked.

The girl with the flute stood there in the grass at the side of the road, looking down at me as she played her instrument.

"Please," I said. "Can you help me get out of here?" I tried to unbuckle my seat belt, but my entire weight pushed down against it. I couldn't brace myself with my bad shoulder. "I need a hand here."

The girl kept playing her flute.

Are you kidding me?

Then, still playing, she stepped closer to me. As she trilled, her lips pursed, fingers flying, she reached out a foot and put it through the open window, poking my bare stomach with her dirty toes. None too gently, I might add.

What the hell? Was she brain damaged?

Even though I was in pain and wanted to bawl, I realized Flute Girl might be the only thing that stood between my staying in that car forever or my getting help and making it home.

So I swallowed the swelling animosity at her utter ignorance or absolute lack of compassion or *whatever* her issue was, forced half a smile onto my face, and injected an entire dose of false cheer into my voice. "Yeah, I'm kind of stuck here. Driving too fast. Stupid, I know. But I'm pretty sure I'm hurt, so if you could . . ."

At last, Flute Girl stopped playing.

". . . help me get . . ." My inane rambling tapered off.

She slowly lowered her flute and squatted next to the car. We were nearly eye to eye, although I was still upside down and beginning to see spots. She set the flute down on the grass beside her, so gently, laying it there as if it were made of eggshells.

The tenderness of her actions sent a wave of relief through me. I let out a breath.

She's going to help me.

Flute Girl's gaze rested on the flute, as if reluctant to leave the precious instrument for even a moment. She sighed before turning her full attention to me.

"That's it, I think if you help me unhook . . ." I trailed off.

Because that was when I noticed something, a small detail that, despite my raging headache and the pain in my shoulder and the barely faded terror at *rolling my freaking car*, managed to cause a chill to run up my aching spine.

I'd been wrong about her eyes.

They weren't the eyes of someone who was angry or pissed off or slightly annoyed.

Those eyes were just plain mean.

Then Flute Girl smiled at me, revealing a gap between her two front teeth, a smile that would have been endearing on anyone else in the world. On anyone else, that smile would have been reassuring, telling me, *Everything will be okay. You are safe.*

But on her? That smile was god-awful sinister.

She picked up a stick about as thick as a good-sized snake and wielded it like a baseball bat, her fists tightening around it with none of the care she showered on her flute. And before my vision started swimming and I passed out, the last thing I saw was Flute Girl swinging that club straight at my head.

2

"OH-*LIV*-EE-AAAH! OH-*LIV*-EE-AAAAAAAAH!"

Mom?

My mother was the only one who called me by my full name anymore. Well, she and our family dentist, who had known me since I was two. My readers—the world—knew me as Livvy Flynn.

And by *world*, I mainly meant the thirty-two countries where the foreign language rights for my series had been licensed. When the first few translations sold, I had posters made of the covers. But as the deals kept rolling in, I gave up. Instead, I had a juniper bookcase made for all the foreign editions.

My talent and fame didn't exactly pour in much-needed money to my family. We were already pretty well off. I mean, my dad was an oral surgeon and my mom used to be a lawyer, so I would've gotten into the best dorm on their dime alone. But they supported me from the start. I started writing pretty seriously when I was twelve, and when it was clear I had a knack for it, my parents encouraged me to keep at it. When I turned fourteen, Mom told me about a boot camp for novelists in Los Angeles. Although it sounded pretty cool, I hadn't written anything that long yet and wasn't sure I wanted to go. But Mom insisted. Of course she paid for it, as well as our rooms at the Beverly Hilton, so I didn't even know how expensive it was until I overheard a woman say she took money out of her kid's college fund to attend.

Everyone else there was female and old. In fact, I was practically the only person under thirty. Only a man would have felt more out of place. I wanted to sneak out, go find my mom, and have her take me to Disneyland or the beach or *anywhere else* for the next three days.

But then, as we all broke up into critique groups and got to sharing our story ideas, I looked around at those housewives and waitresses and listened to them as they jabbered about finding each other and sharing the same dream. It took me about half a day to realize I didn't want to be like them: half their lives over, still waiting and hoping for a far-fetched fantasy that was never going to happen.

In that moment, I realized how much I did want to be a writer. But I didn't want it to be simply a fantasy, something I gushed about like all those women. I wanted it to be reality. I would *make* it a reality.

So I decided right then and there not to wait until I was old. I would write a bestseller before I was out of high school.

And I did.

On the flight home from the boot camp, I began *The Caul and the Coven*, the first book in a series about twin teenage sisters born into an old family in Portland. Their mother died in childbirth, so they live with their grandfather. One day they discover a book in the attic, their mother trapped in the pages. The only way to release her is to find the entire set of books, each guarded by a witch, and bring them together. The series is about their journey to find the books, and of course they find love and encounter danger along the way as they struggle to release their mother.

"Oh-*liv*-ee-aaah!"

That is definitely not my mom.

The voice was high-pitched, the voice of a child. A girl.

A vision of Flute Girl popped into my head, and I forced my eyes open, but everything was fuzzy, revealing only blurry whiteness.

A ceiling?

No longer hanging upside down in the ruins of my Audi, I lay on something soft.

A bed? Had help come? Was I in a hospital?

I shut my eyes.

Thank God.

My head was killing me. *Advil, please.*

The ambulance crew, or whoever rescued me, would have found my purse. My driver's license bore my legal name, Olivia Louise Flynn. Of course the nurses would call me Olivia. My nurse was young, that's all.

I opened my eyes again and tried to focus. On the three sides of the room visible from my vantage point, shelves covered the top half. A desk was pushed against one wall while another had two folding chairs beside a table with several blue-topped clear plastic tubs piled on top.

What kind of hospital was this?

The place looked more like somebody's scrapbook room.

"Hello?" Talking made my head hurt. Hopefully I wouldn't have to speak again. I shut my eyes.

"Olivia?" This voice was different from the other, deeper and older. Still feminine, though.

My eyes opened to a woman's face peering down at me. Blond curly hair fell to her shoulders, and she was rather pretty, with a dimple in her chin, but a lot of wrinkles around her eyes. She was probably a cheerleader in high school before she went into nursing. Before she got old. Before she got all those frown lines.

"You're awake." Her voice was flat, emotionless.

Shouldn't a medical professional be somewhat *pleased* that the victim of a rollover was awake and speaking and not *deceased*?

"My head hurts."

She straightened up and put her hands on her hips. "I suppose it does." Her outfit consisted of jeans and a faded aqua T-shirt emblazoned with a crossbow and the words *Mrs. Daryl Dixon*. Her black bra peeked out of a small hole on the right side.

A *Walking Dead* shirt. Odd attire for a nurse.

My heart started to pound.

She's not a nurse.

I am not in a hospital.

"Please, I need to get to a hospital." *Please.*

Mrs. Daryl Dixon scratched her head. "Oh, I called 911." She held up the palm of her left hand, a gesture of apology. "Sometimes it takes them a while to get out here." She set a hand on my left shoulder, my *hurt* shoulder, and pressed.

I screamed at the instant shot of agony. Unable to help it, I burst into tears.

She let go immediately. "Oh. You *are* hurt. I wondered." Quite honestly, Mrs. Dixon sounded like she didn't give a crap whether I was hurt or not.

Where the hell am I? Who is this witch?

"Please," I said through my tears. "Call my mom. My phone is in my purse. . . ." But she already knew that, didn't she? If she knew my name, then she had already been in my purse, had already gone through at least my wallet to see my driver's license. My heart pounded faster.

"It's okay," she said. "Like I said, the ambulance should be here before too long."

My eyes closed, shutting her out—*for God's sake, shut up!*—but she kept talking.

"I suppose you aren't used to waiting for anything, are you, Olivia? You probably get whatever you want, exactly when you want it." She sighed. "You have no idea, do you?"

What did she mean by that? Did she just assume that, due to my expensive car? That I probably had money?

Or did she know who I was?

Doubtful.

Flute Girl was too young to read my books, probably too stupid as well, and Mrs. Dixon didn't strike me as much of a reader.

Should I tell her who I am?

Would it mean anything if they knew I was a world-famous author?

Somehow, I thought not.

I pretended to be asleep or passed out or whatever kind of unconscious state was plausible for someone who had recently rolled her car and probably had a concussion.

No, actually I *wasn't* used to waiting, and *yes*, I usually did get what I wanted.

And right now, Mrs. Daryl Freaking Dixon, I want you to stop talking, and I want the ambulance to get here, and I want to get some pain medicine, and I want to get my shoulder fixed, and I want my mom, and I WANT TO GO HOME. . . .

The door creaked.

I sucked in a breath and froze. Was she leaving?

"Mama."

The voice. The one I'd first heard say my name.

Flute Girl? Was Mrs. Dixon her mother?

My heart sank as I tried to stay motionless.

"Is she dead?" Flute Girl sounded a little too excited at the prospect of my checking out for good. Maybe that had been her intent when she came at me with that club.

Did this woman—apparently her mother—know?

Something poked me in my cheek.

My eyes fluttered open.

Flute Girl stood next to her mother, both of them looking down at me.

Gathering every ounce of ornery still in my possession, I growled, "I'm not dead."

Flute Girl reached out again to poke me. There was dirt under her fingernails. I reached over with my good hand and slapped hers away. The movement sent a fresh course of pain up my bad shoulder, yet I managed to growl, "Get your filthy hands off me."

Both of them took a step back. Flute Girl crossed her arms as her mother simply frowned at me.

"Well," said Mrs. Dixon. "Maybe you need some time by yourself until you can figure out how to apologize to my daughter."

"Apologize?" I nearly spit out the word. "Are you for real? After what she did? She hit me with a stick!"

Mrs. Dixon looked down at Flute Girl, who shrugged half-heartedly with one shoulder, then turned her gaze to me. Her eyes narrowed. "What my daughter did was come and get me and tell me there was an accident. Then we both got you out of the wreck and brought you here. Do you know how hard that was?"

"You didn't have to do that!" My face burned as I cried and shouted, which sent fissures of pain out from my shoulder, but I couldn't make myself stop. "All you had to do was call

911!" And it dawned on me that for whatever reason, she hadn't called them. Not at all. "Just give me my phone! Let me call myself!" The yelling killed my head, and I had to shut my eyes against the tears pouring out. My pounding heart seriously made my brain hurt.

Just breathe.

The woman's voice droned on, berating me. "Are you this ungrateful to everyone? Or just people who pull you out of cars and bring you into their homes?"

Breathe. I scrunched my eyes shut tighter against the swelling pain and frustration and anger. *Stay rational. This woman is crazy, and you have to stay calm.*

I opened my eyes back up and tried to smile as I sucked up to her. "Thank you so much for that. But I really think I should let you all get back to what you were doing before I came along. You have been . . . so kind." I almost choked on those words, but I kept going, hoping it would help. "I'm sure you'll be happy to get me out of here and on my way. So maybe you could try 911 one more time." And then, the addition of the one thing that most certainly would seal my fate. "I'd be happy to pay you for your trouble."

Which it did, seal my fate, that is, because Mrs. Dixon's face clouded over, a sudden thunderstorm on a previously partly sunny day. She grabbed the arm of Flute Girl and whipped around to the door.

Desperation choked me as I cried, "Wait! Where are you going?"

Flute Girl went through the door, and the woman turned

back around to face me, glowering. "You think you can buy anything, don't you? Well you can't buy me." And she left, slamming the door behind her.

"And no one is coming for you!"

There was a very distinctive *Click!*

Did she lock me in? Holy crap, she locked me in.

I yelled, "You can't do this!" I rolled onto my good side, curled up my legs, and dropped them over the side of the bed. I used my momentum to sit up. "Ah!" The swift stab of pain in my shoulder sent a flurry of white snow across my vision. My balance wavered.

I dropped my head and took a deep breath. As my gaze eventually cleared, I found myself staring down at my feet on the green indoor/outdoor carpeting that covered the floor. My bare feet.

Where were my shoes?

I glanced at my right wrist. My MedicAlert bracelet and gold and silver Rolex were still there. My clothes as well: black leggings, camisole, sweater.

But my shoes, my $300 black Italian leather flats, were missing.

All the more reason to find out what the hell was going on.

I counted to three and stood up.

The white snow returned, but this time as a blizzard that refused to clear. Before I could sit back down on the bed, I promptly fainted.

3

MY DREAMS WERE of McGrath's Fish House, a restaurant in Bend where we went nearly every Sunday after church. For an appetizer, my dad always ordered the bruschetta topped with a tapenade and tomatoes and shrimp and a balsamic vinegar reduction glaze. He reeked of garlic for days afterward. The stench seeped out his pores. Once when his breath sang of garlic, my dad had tried to kiss my mom, but she playfully fended him off.

I tried that appetizer one time. But the taste of garlic lingered in my mouth the rest of the day, making me put my hand in front of my mouth in case anyone got near enough to smell my breath. I didn't exactly have to worry about someone trying to kiss me. Well, at the moment anyway. Because I knew exactly who I wanted to kiss.

My boyfriend, Rory, lived in Illinois, half a continent away. We didn't get the chance to see each other much—actually we had never even met in person—but he promised to meet me when my November book tour stopped in Chicago.

Before Rory, I didn't have a lot of friends my age. Actually, make that no friends. I started writing my series the summer before freshman year of high school. Because I was so immersed in it, we decided as a family that homeschooling would make much more sense than traditional school. So I signed up for an online charter, and Mom resigned from her law firm to stay home with me. I knew how much of a sacrifice that was for her, because she was the sole "minority" partner. The birth mother was an unknown Vietnamese girl; birth father, an unknown GI with some black heritage. Luckily, in the waning days of the Vietnam War, some kindhearted soul had stuck her on a plane evacuating orphans to the US, where she'd been adopted by a wonderful family.

So Mom grew up in Portland, went to Lewis & Clark Law School, and worked hard to make partner in a Bend law firm made up of white guys. She assured me nothing would make her more fulfilled than staying home with me.

I felt guilty about it at first, but soon it was clear how much more relaxed she was when she didn't have to go to work all the time.

And it was all worth it because shortly after that came my book deal, and that was that: school for two hours in the morning, writing the rest of the day.

After my first book tour when I was sixteen, Rory sent a message to my Facebook fan page, introducing himself. He said he'd been at one of my appearances, but was too embarrassed to meet me so he had his mother get his book signed for him. His picture was nice; he had short dark hair and blue eyes and a charming smile with dimples. I wrote back, telling him I remembered signing the name Rory. That was a lie; I didn't remember at all, but I didn't want to make him feel bad. Actually, more than that? I wanted to say something that would make him feel good, would maybe make him want to write back. Which he did.

He was the first boy my age I'd ever corresponded with. We discovered we had so many things in common: He loved Edgar Allan Poe as much as I did. I told him about the huge poster I had of Poe up in my room, and he had the same one. And we were both deathly allergic to bee stings. He wore a MedicAlert bracelet, too.

After a month, we started talking on the phone. Secretly, of course, because I didn't think my parents would approve of me spending so much time with a boy they had never met. And only on Sunday nights because he had six AP courses and had to get a 4.0 if he stood any chance of getting a scholarship, so he spent almost every waking moment studying.

I wanted to tell him that I could pay for his college so he wouldn't have to study so hard and could spend more time talking with me. But I wasn't sure how he'd take that. (As if my parents would even have let me.) And then we began to Skype. Well, sort of, because the camera was broken on his laptop and he couldn't afford to get it fixed. So I couldn't see him, but he could see me.

He was the first person who ever told me I was beautiful.

I wasn't *beautiful*, I knew that. But my skin was a nice mix of Mom and pasty-white Dad, and my hair was good, finally. My nose wasn't too big and my eyes were a lovely brown and my teeth were white and even. I wished I looked more like my mom, but my lips were kind of thin, like my dad's, and I knew that even on a great day, I wouldn't pass much beyond "kinda pretty."

But when Rory told me that I was beautiful? My heart pounded and I blushed. And I would make sure that when we did meet, and we did get a chance to kiss for the first time, I would not eat any garlic beforehand.

Garlic. Why was I dreaming about garlic?

I opened my eyes.

Flute Girl knelt next to me on the floor, orange stains on her chin, breathing garlic breath all over me.

I started to sit up and the pain in my shoulder made me freeze and fall back onto the floor with a groan. I lay there and tried not to focus on the throbbing.

She scooted back, not taking her eyes off me as she called out, "Mama! Oh-liv-ee-ah is awake."

I wanted so badly to reach up and smack my name off her lips, tell her never to say it again. But all I could do was lie there, bracing myself until the wave of agony receded enough that I could start breathing again.

Footsteps neared and Mrs. Daryl Dixon walked into the room, holding a plate of noodles and marinara sauce and a slice of garlic bread. She smiled. "Well, good. Just in time for dinner."

Through gritted teeth, I said, "I need medical attention, not spaghetti."

She tilted her head slightly. "But you must be hungry."

21

Let this be a dream. I shut my eyes. *Let it be some stupid dream.*

Then the stench of garlic again, as Flute Girl's breath puffed on my face.

"Get away."

I opened my eyes. Flute Girl sidled away from me, like one of those weird slack-limbed creatures in a horror movie, her pigtails swinging from side to side as her skinny arms and legs drove her backward. Really, it wasn't much of a stretch to envision that pint-sized asshat as a spawn of evil, come to kill us all.

Mrs. Dixon set the plate down and stood above me, looking down. Her hair fell around her face as she shook her head. "You probably shouldn't try to get up on your own." She looked at her daughter. "Help me get her back in bed."

Mrs. Dixon reached for my good arm as Flute Girl headed for my bad one.

"No!" I straightened out my right arm and thrust my palm at her. "Don't! Not the bad side—please!"

Flute Girl didn't listen. Instead, she gripped my bad arm with both her grimy hands and twisted.

The pain was a sharp knife slicing through my shoulder. I screamed and tried to hit Flute Girl with my other arm, but her mother already had a firm hold on it. So I kicked out with my legs, which did nothing but make the pain worse. They dragged me off the floor by my arms as I screamed.

Flute Girl backed up onto the bed, still wrenching my shoulder.

"Stop it! You're hurting me!" I began to dissolve into ugly crying. "Stop! Oh please, stop!"

Flute Girl finally let go, and Mrs. Dixon shoved me so that I found myself facedown on the bed, my bad shoulder twisted under me. I bawled at the pain, unable to move. Tears mixed with snot smeared onto the bed.

I gathered all the strength I had left and pushed off with my good arm, until I was lying flat on my back. Then I maneuvered until my bad shoulder was in the air, as close to elevating it as I could get.

The sobs took away my breath, and between gasps I said, "You've got to get me to a hospital." At first I wondered if they had even heard me. *Are they gone?*

I rolled my head to the side. Both of them still stood there, watching me.

Flute Girl wrinkled her nose. "Her face is a mess."

Mrs. Dixon walked over to the desk and brought back a box of tissues. She pushed it at me. "Here. Clean yourself up." Then she took Flute Girl's hand and led her to the door. Flute Girl walked through, but her mother turned back to me. "Maybe you'll be hungry for breakfast." Then she picked up the plate of spaghetti and shut the door after her.

Click!

I lay there, sobbing, until the only sounds coming out of me were ragged sighs. My God, I was in a freaking Stephen King novel. Only in *Misery*, Annie Wilkes gave the dude painkillers.

I reached for the tissue and blew my nose with one hand as

23

best as I could. I didn't plan on hanging around long enough to let Mrs. Dixon start hacking off any of my extremities, that was for sure.

No more crying.

I wiped my face.

Crying isn't going to get you out of here.

I didn't know what Mrs. Dixon and Flute Girl were up to. Were they insane? Or was this some game they were playing so I would *think* they were insane?

Because it was abundantly clear that they had not called anyone: not my parents or the authorities or the first responders. Didn't Oregon have some sort of Good Samaritan law? Whatever it was, they had broken it. No phone call made it clear they meant to do me harm.

Which meant it was me against them.

"So no more crying."

I swallowed, wiped my nose, and sniffled.

"No more." I shuddered. "You have to be strong if you're going to fight." I kicked myself for not taking the food, because I was hungry. And thirsty.

"You're smart. Do what you do best."

I'd written my first novel fairly quickly, going where the story led me. But since then, I researched each new book. And then I outlined, meticulously. Sometimes I spent months on the outline and then whipped out the novel itself in a few weeks. I didn't mind spending time and effort on the preparation, and maybe that fortitude would be my salvation.

I needed to plot. To plan. Sure, at the moment they had the

upper hand physically, but there was no doubt in my mind that I was smarter. I had to think my way out of this.

Mrs. Dixon had mentioned dinner. I had no idea what time it was, although it was dark outside. In the summer, that meant it had to be at least eight, possibly nine, maybe even later.

The windows were small and high up on the wall.

Could I escape?

Sucking in my breath at the pain, I slowly sat up and slid over to the side of the bed. Then, forcing myself to take it inch by inch, I grabbed the headboard for support and stood up. I felt wobbly, so I sat back down until my head felt clear enough to try again.

I stood up, took a few deep breaths. Woozy, for sure, but better than earlier. I shuffled to the closest window. It was about a foot over my head, but I could see outside. The glow from a big yard light illuminated part of a white-flowered bush and the side of a red wooden building of some kind.

Given the height and size of the window, I had to be in a basement. Getting through the window, if I could figure out how to do it, would be a tight squeeze.

Oh, and one more thing:

Getting out that window is gonna hurt.

And so would what came after: trying to find my way to the road and then walking, for who knew how far, barefoot. And they might come after me, try to drag me back.

I would have to be prepared to fight.

Climbing through the window, escaping, maybe having to

fight my way out of there . . . all of that would take strength, strength I did not have yet.

Plus, I wasn't stupid. I'd seen it time and time again in movies: The captive tries to escape right away, before she thinks things through. She discovers her captor has left her an out, an opening, and she takes it. But she *always* takes it too soon, and she *always* gets caught. I supposed she has to— otherwise the movie would be over in the first half hour.

But that was a mistake I was not going to make. I knew I might only get one shot, so I was going to make sure my escape was foolproof.

I was going to take my time.

Since I was finally standing, I had a better view of the room. There was another door. At a glacial pace, holding my bad arm motionless with my good, I limped over and pulled it open.

A small bathroom.

Which I hadn't realized I seriously needed until I noticed the toilet. It took me a while, given that I was minus one arm. I sat there, looking at everything. Save for a plastic pump bottle of Bath & Body Works coconut lime hand soap, there wasn't much. When I finished, I slurped water from the faucet for a long time.

Then I looked at myself in the cheap metal mirror. My dark hair had drifted out of the pretty French braids my mom had done around my head. My face seemed puffy, and there were bruises, probably from where I hit the steering wheel when I crashed. Which reminded me that when all this was over, I would have to write a strongly worded letter to the CEO of Audi about their crap air bags.

Or maybe the bruise was from when Flute Girl hit me.

Rory wouldn't think I was beautiful, not if he could see me now.

I blew out a breath and shut my eyes. I needed to rest. I needed to eat. I needed to get strong before I could try to escape.

I opened my eyes and told my reflection, "I will. I will."

Standing there, leaning on the sink with one good hand, I continued, "You need a plan. A good one. You need . . . let's see. A list. You need a list."

My stomach growled.

Passing up the spaghetti had been seriously stupid on my part. I added it to my growing list of regrets, the first of which was, obviously, ever leaving home in the first place.

I started to feel light-headed, so I made my way back to the bed and gingerly lay back down. I breathed out and took comfort in the softness of the bedspread and the mattress, willing my heartbeat to slow and my mind to relax.

"You always dwell on the bad. Find something good."

I turned my head so my cheek was on the pillow. I sniffed.

That was one thing to be grateful for. My captors could have been less hygienic, and left me lying on a dirt floor somewhere, with a bucket for a toilet and vermin crawling all over me as I slept. Instead, I was lying on a nice bed with covers and a decent pillow that smelled like a sunny day in a meadow.

Lucky me.

"Tomorrow. Tomorrow I make a list and plan my escape."

I shut my eyes.

For now, rest . . .

4

THE SUN STREAMING in the windows woke me up. My first movements made me gasp; in addition to the jab of pain in my shoulder, the rest of my body was so stiff and sore that even blinking hurt.

My exhaustion should have been sufficient to knock me out for the night, but sleep had been fitful. The pain in my shoulder was smothering, and I had to lie absolutely still, taking long, slow breaths, to keep it from consuming me.

I refused to cry out to Flute Girl and her witch of a mother. They knew that one simple squeeze of my shoulder would bring me to my knees. Which, apparently, was exactly where they wanted me.

Really?

But why?

I had tried not to go there, to breach the constant barrage of *whys*: *Why didn't they call 911? Why did Flute Girl hit me with a branch? Why did they bring me into their house? And why the hell are they keeping me locked in the basement?*

I sighed, deep enough that I had to grit my teeth and hold

my breath until the pain passed. I reached up with my right arm and ran my fingers lightly over my bad shoulder until I felt what I was looking for. A lump.

My shoulder was dislocated. I would have bet money on it. I'd researched the injury for a book once, and it mentioned pain with movement and also a bump or lump. Problem was, there was no way for me to put it back in myself, and I knew they weren't about to help me. The best thing would be to stabilize it somehow. I should have been icing it and taking Tylenol or Advil or *freaking Vicodin*. But those options weren't exactly available to me at the moment.

As long as I lay on my good side, at least the shoulder was elevated a bit.

My lips were dry, and my throat was parched, but I needed to psych myself up to make the trek to the bathroom.

Until then, I would work on my list.

First things first: escape route. That had to be first, right?

No, maybe not. Because something might prevent me from getting to the escape route. Or be in my way while I was taking the escape route. I would have to drag something over to the window to stand on, and I might get interrupted while doing that.

So . . . I needed a weapon.

My eyes wandered around the room. There were shelves . . . books . . . papers on the desk. . . .

Crafty crap. Scrapbooking supplies.

Ten to one they had already removed any sharp objects.

So a rainbow glitter gel pen maybe? Jabbed in an eye?

But that brought up a new question.

What was the purpose of my weapon? The end goal? Exactly how far was I willing to go?

Was I aiming to simply stun?

Temporarily disable?

Permanently maim?

Would I kill if I had to?

When it came down to that moment, that moment when I needed to escape and Flute Girl and her mother were standing in my way, could I use my weapon against them?

I didn't know what I was capable of. At that moment, I wasn't strong enough to kill a bug if I wanted to.

I sighed.

Wait on the weapon.

In the movies, the captive always makes the mistake of leaving before she has enough intel. I needed to know more. I needed to know their routines, what time they got up, what time they went to bed. What they did during the day.

Did they have activities that made a lot of noise? Vacuuming? Running the dishwasher while they watched a movie so they had to turn up the television really loud?

Too bad Flute Girl wasn't Tuba Girl. *That* would've covered up any sound I had to make.

Diversion.

If I picked a time when they were in the middle of whatever it was they did—bath? shower? trip to the grocery store?

church? (yeah, that one was doubtful)—then I would have a better chance of buying myself some time. Of course, I had the disadvantage of being locked in this stupid room.

One thing for sure: They needed to think I was in as bad a shape as possible. I mean, I *was* in terrible shape, so I didn't have to fake that. But if they thought that I was truly incapacitated, not capable of even moving myself about, they might relax their guard.

So as bad off as I was, they needed to think I was worse. No, they needed to *believe* I was worse.

And then, when they left the room, I could sneak over to the door and listen for something that would help me escape. But I needed to eliminate—or at the very least, curb—my weaknesses. I glanced at my shoulder, obviously low on the asset list.

I sat up and slowly maneuvered out of my sweater. Then I flopped one sleeve over my left shoulder and pulled it under. I tucked my left arm in close and across my stomach. I tied the sleeves with my good hand, sticking a sleeve in my mouth to help me pull the sweater tight, immobilizing my arm and my shoulder.

Click!

I quickly shut my eyes and slid back down, letting my jaw fall open as I took deep, even breaths.

The door opened, and someone took a few cautious steps into the room. There was a slight jingle. A dog collar?

No.

Bracelets?

I hadn't noticed any jewelry on either of them. But then I had been out of it the day before. That couldn't happen again.

Vigilant. I would have to be aware of *everything*, hear *everything*. Absorb and remember *everything*.

I took a deep, loud breath and moved a bit. Then I opened my eyes.

Mrs. Dixon stood about five feet away, staring down at me. She wore a smock with red-and-black flowers on it, black scrub pants, and shiny red patent leather clogs. In her left hand was an orange-and-black Oregon State University lanyard with a key on it. *Oh, it figures that she's a Beaver fan.*

A small key. Like to a padlock? Was that what she locked me in with? Somehow, that made me feel worse. I hadn't thought about it before, but why *did* someone put a lock on the outside of a door? To keep someone from getting in? Or to keep someone from getting out?

I shivered, and she noticed I was awake.

Her head tilted a little, as if she was considering something. "You're up."

"Yeah." Hopefully that one word had sounded laborious, my voice feeble, like the act of getting it out was a strain for my shattered self.

Mrs. Dixon said, "I see you felt perky enough to make yourself a sling." She glanced at the open bathroom door. "And get yourself out of bed."

Crap. Livvy! Why didn't you shut the door?

I nodded slightly. "Last night." I swallowed, making a big show of the effort. "I'm not sure I could do it now. I feel so . . .

33

weak." I hoped I wasn't laying it on too thick. But then again, I would bet that my intelligence outranked hers.

She said, "You need to eat. Keep up your strength."

The words didn't sound like she was musing aloud. She sounded confident, like it was an order. Did she work in health care? From the looks of her outfit, I thought maybe she did.

She smiled a bit. "I'll be right back."

Mrs. Dixon shut the door behind her.

Click!

Definitely a padlock.

I blew out the breath I didn't know I'd been holding. What did she think I needed to keep my strength up for? Did she need me strong? Did she—

You are so stupid.

Ransom. Despite her previous freak-out at my mention of money, there could be no other reason. Plain and simple: They knew who I was, and they had kidnapped me.

With the lock on the outside of the door, maybe this was premeditated. They had seen the car, my shoes—the $300 shoes that were no longer either on my feet or anywhere in sight—and then they had probably dug in my purse. They'd found my ID, either recognized the name or looked me up, and then they'd decided to get some money out of it.

I racked my brain to remember anything about kidnapping, fact *or* fiction. Kidnappers usually took pretty good care of the victims, didn't they? They needed them to stay in good shape for the exchange, right?

The exchange. Had she already called my parents and set a ransom amount? Was she simply waiting for them to pay?

Maybe I should go ahead and tell her that they would pay whatever it took. Hell, I had money; *I* could cut her a check, then and there.

She came back in holding a plate, and I decided not to say anything. Instead, I would lie back, wait, and let *her* provide some information for once.

My hunger had put my senses on overload, and I smelled . . . *garlic?*

Mrs. Dixon set the plate of spaghetti and garlic bread from last night on the dresser next to the bed. She nodded her head at the bathroom. "I guess you can get yourself in there if you want a drink of water."

Before I had a chance to say anything, she was out the door, locking the padlock behind her.

I frowned at the plate of spaghetti. "What the hell?" I painfully inched my way to a sitting position so I could see the plate. Maybe I was wrong. Maybe it wasn't the same plate.

I slowly reached out, my hand hovering above the food. Ice cold. "Are you *serious?*"

Apparently she had absolutely no idea how a kidnap victim was supposed to be treated.

I maneuvered my way to the edge of the bed so my right hand could reach the plate. Balancing it on my lap, I took a moment to appraise the meal.

The butter on the garlic bread had congealed. With one

finger, I poked at the slice. Rock hard around the edges, still semi-soft in the middle, saturated by pooled garlic and butter. I dug some out with my finger and stuck the frigid lump in my mouth.

I started to gag, but slapped my hand over my mouth.

You need to eat.

I forced myself to chew and swallow. "Gah." I shook my head. But then I pried out some more bread, continuing until all that was left was the stony shell of crust. The noodles and marinara sauce looked unappetizing as hell. I wasn't a big fan of meat, especially hamburger that had sat out all night, but the chill of the plate reassured me. At least it had been in the fridge and not growing bacteria that would consume my organs while I slept.

Any of the noodles not covered by sauce were shriveled and brittle. I twisted the fork in the middle of the pile until it was laden with soft noodles and sauce. I stuck the food in my mouth and chewed. Not as bad as the bread, for some reason. I swallowed, and then got another bite.

I ate cold pizza, right? What was the difference?

I took another bite. While I was chewing, I attempted to move the dried noodles out of the way. The fork slipped out of my hand. I grabbed for it, but my right knee shifted. The plate slid right off my lap and landed with a crash on the green indoor/outdoor carpet, which apparently wasn't enough of a cushion because the plate burst into pieces. Spaghetti flew all over the floor.

Click!

I stiffened.

Had she been standing out there the whole time, listening?

The door slammed open, black-and-orange lanyard with the key clutched in Mrs. Dixon's hand. Her glare soaked in the mess at my feet. Her face reddened as her eyes narrowed at me. "Ungrateful. Little. Bitch."

I blurted out, "It was an accident!"

She strode toward me, eyes narrow slits. "Disrespectful—"

I held out my right arm. "I was eating, I swear!"

Her hand swung at me, and I ducked, trying to avoid the blow. It landed on my good shoulder, not that hard, but I shrieked anyway.

"Clean it up!" Mrs. Dixon screamed. "You won't get anything more until you clean it up!"

My heart pounded, and my face got hot. My eyes filled with tears as I glared back at her. "What do you want from me?" I swallowed, trying to gather my voice, which seemed to abandon me. "Just tell me what you want. Money? I'll give you money. My parents will give you money!"

Suddenly petulant, she took a step back, her mouth forming a small O. Her forehead wrinkled. "Is that what you think? That I am doing this for money?"

I nodded. "Why else would you keep me locked up, not call 911? I was in an accident, for God's sake. I'm hurt." And then I realized I wasn't so much afraid of her, although I should have been. Instead, I was pissed as hell. "Are you even aware of Good Samaritan laws? I'm pretty sure you're breaking every freaking one."

A smile played at her lips. Then she laughed, so hard her eyes filled with tears and she leaned over, setting her hand on her knees.

What the hell did she find so funny? I sniffled and wiped my nose.

Still half laughing, Mrs. Dixon finally stood back up. "Oh my God. I told you last night, I don't want your money."

"Then what?" I shook my head. "I don't know what you want from me."

She crossed her arms, eyes once again serious. "I want you to admit what you did. I want you to admit that you"— suddenly she gulped in a breath—"No. No *you* have to figure it out. *You* have to remember. Or it doesn't mean anything."

What was she talking about? Something I did after my accident? Before it? Had she seen me driving too fast? Was she worried I might have slammed into Flute Girl?

Maybe she should tell her little freak-show offspring not to play in the road.

"Remember what?" My voice was calmer, only because I was doing everything in my power to sound rational. "I have no idea what you're talking about."

She turned and walked toward the door.

"Wait!" I didn't want her to leave. I didn't want to be locked in again. I did want to do what she needed me to do. Because I did want to go home. "Please. I will totally do whatever you want. *Say* whatever you want me to say."

Mrs. Dixon whirled around to face me. "I told you that wouldn't mean anything! Don't you get it?"

"Then tell me." I was on the verge of tears yet again. "Tell me what to do so I can go home."

She rested her hand on the doorknob and smiled at me. Then she pointed at the broken plate of spaghetti. "You can start by cleaning that up." Then she left, the click of the padlock sealing me in.

5

THE EXCHANGE WITH Mrs. Dixon left me breathless, my heart pounding, sobs catching in my throat. I wiped my face with the back of my hand. I needed to calm down. Even though it would hurt to get back up, I lay down on the bed and got as comfortable as possible.

My eyes closed.

I *would* clean up the mess. Later. After I rested and got some strength back. And I suspected they would leave me alone for a while, so there should be plenty of time.

A few deep, cleansing breaths made me feel a little better, although my head was killing me nearly as much as my shoulder.

What had she meant? What did I have to apologize for?

The weird thing was, although she didn't come out and say so, Mrs. Dixon acted like she knew me. Knew who I was.

She could have, definitely. Maybe she had read my books. My photograph wasn't on the covers, but there were shots of me online from signings. If she did know about me, she would have recognized my name if she had looked at my driver's license.

Maybe I was totally wrong about her, and perhaps she had attended one of the conferences where I gave the keynote. Or maybe one of my bookstore appearances in Portland or Bend or Salem.

But if that was the case, what could I have possibly done to make her mad enough to kidnap me?

Because seriously, once she got caught, she would be in deep trouble. Deep. She would get thrown in jail, and her kid would be taken away from her.

I could think of nothing to warrant that kind of a risk.

The events I attended gave me no opportunity to screw up that bad. At conferences, I typically did a panel with other authors or maybe a First Pages event with my editor, where participants read us the first pages of their novels and then we gave our first impressions. If I liked what they read, I was honest. And if I didn't like it, I was diplomatic, always careful to find something nice to say. I lied if I had to. So the chance of pissing anyone off at one of those events, in my opinion, was infinitesimal.

Book signings consisted of reading a chapter before signing books. Worst-case scenario was that I could have been crabby or rude or dismissive. But any worse sins were impossible. I was never even alone with anyone; my mom sat on one side and a media escort or an employee of the bookstore sat on the other.

And the conferences? Either my editor was with me or Billy, my agent.

My eyes snapped open.

Billy! Why hadn't I thought of him before?

He had called me on the drive because a German publisher wanted to put my books into paperback. Billy advised holding out for more money but wanted to run the specifics by me first. My cell kept fading in and out on the Santiam Pass, so I said I would call as soon as I arrived at the retreat. Billy told me to make sure that I did because he needed to get back to them on Monday.

So that was Friday. He would have expected me to call him that day, and he knew that I would. Billy was amazing, and I owed him my career. My mom hadn't wanted me to get an agent; she thought that 15 percent of my earnings was too much of a cut. But I would rather have 85 percent of something than 100 percent of nothing. And I'd made the right call. Billy championed my words from the get-go, and we both made a bunch of money because of it.

He would not have let the sun set on Friday without talking to me.

So was it Saturday? Had to be.

When Billy couldn't reach my cell, he would have called my house and talked to my mother. And Mom would have tried to call me, and then she would have gotten worried. She had all the contact information for the retreat.

The retreat!

They had already sent me part of my fee and would have

absolutely flipped when I didn't show up. Among the conference organizers, my mom, and Billy, someone had to realize something was wrong.

They would be searching for me. For my car. And they would find it.

Right?

But how far was my car from where I was now?

Maybe miles.

But Flute Girl had been barefoot. Even with soles of leather—or cloven hooves—she couldn't have been all that far from home. Plus, if they had both dragged me to their house . . .

My car had to be nearby.

And as soon as anyone saw it, they'd call the police. And they would come looking for me.

"They'll find my car." I breathed out, trying to relax. "And then they'll find me. They will."

Outside a motor started up. Gravel crunched, and a vehicle drove by the window. The sound disappeared. I rolled to my right, sat up, and slid off the bed onto my feet, careful to avoid the broken plate. I gimped over to the door and pressed my ear against it. Music and canned laughter drifted down from above, one of those dumb kid shows on television. A chair scraped.

I stood up straight. Mrs. Dixon left Flute Girl home alone?

A door slammed. Then nothing.

I went back to the bed and sat down, perusing the mess of spaghetti and broken china that lay scattered on the green floor. I sighed. I still didn't feel like cleaning up. I leaned over. Maybe some of those noodles were still edible. . . .

A door slammed overhead.

I sat back up.

Quick footsteps covered the floor above and came down the creaky stairs.

I slid off the bed and went over to the door. I pressed my ear to it. "Hello?"

Someone was definitely there. Probably that little freak Flute Girl, messing with me.

Click!

I stepped back, waiting.

The door opened. A small brown cardboard box slid to a stop in front of me as the door slammed.

Click!

I carefully knelt by the box. With the makeshift sling holding my shoulder immobile, my movements didn't hurt as much as they had at first. Or maybe I was adjusting to the constant pain.

Without touching the box, I did a close examination. The edges of the top were tucked snugly together, but there wasn't any tape. With a few fingers of my right hand, I nudged the box.

What was that sound? I bent over the box.

A buzz. Definitely a buzz.

"Oh my God." Flute Girl had brought me my phone! I smiled and murmured, "I take back everything I said about that little jack wagon." I sat down and pushed the box between my two legs, anchoring it. "Don't hang up, don't hang up!" I slipped the fingers of my right hand under the edges in the middle and pulled. The top of the box flopped open all at once, freeing the four angry bees that had been trapped inside.

Two flew straight for my face. I screamed and waved my hand at them. I kept screaming, first because of what my hysterical flailing was doing to my shoulder, but then because of the sting in my right hand as one nailed me.

I kicked the box away and fell back on the floor, then rolled over and painfully crawled to the wall. I got myself upright and leaned against it, legs out straight.

I'd been stung. And I was allergic.

I didn't know exactly what was going to happen. The first and only time I'd been stung was when I was far too little to remember. But when I was ten and put up a fuss about wearing my MedicAlert bracelet, my mother told me, "You nearly died. It was the only time I have ever seen your father cry."

As I leaned there against the wall, a wave of heat coursed over my entire body, like I'd stepped into a furnace. The sting on my hand was already a blister about the size of a quarter. My heart began to race—was it because of my freak-out? Or was an elevated heart rate part of the allergic reaction?

A second later, my breathing grew rapid and shallow.

I screamed, "Help! Please!"

My vision swirled a bit, and my heartbeat sped up even more. I shut my eyes for a moment. "Calm down, calm down." When I opened them, my hand was red and swollen, already a third larger than my other hand. I tried yelling again. "Somebody! Please!"

My throat felt funny. Tickly. I swallowed once, and then tried again, but a knot thickened there, partially blocking my swallows. And it began to hamper my breathing.

Click!

The door opened. Flute Girl stood there, wearing a dirty gray Mickey Mouse shirt and a nasty grin on her face.

I managed to spit out a whisper. "You little bitch."

She shrugged and backed out, shutting the door.

Click!

I tried to get my feet under me, possibly stand up. But my legs trembled and wobbled, then gave out. I collapsed onto my right side. The four bees lazily circled overhead as I lay there.

Bzzzzzzzzzzzzzz.

Nasty suckers probably wondered how long it would take for me to die.

My breaths turned to wheezes, high pitched. My lips and nose tingled.

Bzzzzzzzzzzzzz.

Vaguely, I caught the crunch of tires on gravel.

I squeezed in a breath, which only half entered my oxygen-starved body.

Bzzzzzzzzzzzzz.

A door slammed.

I squeezed in another breath. It felt like a fourth of the air I needed.

Bzzzzzzzzzzzzzz.

Faint voices murmured overhead.

I breathed again. Tried anyway. Barely any air that time.

Bzzzzzzzzzzzzzz.

Footsteps on the stairs.

Click!

The door swung open.

"Oh, balls." Mrs. Daryl Dixon stood there, staring at me.

I reached up a hand to her, with only enough breath for one word:

"Epi."

She whirled around and disappeared, leaving the door open.

Oh, would that I had enough energy to do something about that . . .

I closed my eyes and rolled flat on my back.

Calm down, calm down.

Bzzzzzzzzzzzzzz.

Breathe.

Innnnnnnn.

Ouuuut.

Bzzzzzzzzzzzzzz.

Innnnn.

Ouut.

Bzzzzzzzzzzzzzz.

In—

In—

In—

That one caught.

47

No more breaths.

And no more air.

My eyes snapped open, my mouth shutting and closing like a pathetic guppy. I was a fish, stranded on the beach, aching for water.

Bzzzzzzzzzzzzzz.

How apropos, that the bees' mindless droning was about to sing me out of existence. I had breathed my last and was going to die sprawled on the floor of a strange basement. My gaze darkened around the edges as my eyes brimmed with tears. As much as I wished for air, my lungs remained empty.

No one would ever know what happened to me.

Bzzz.

A blurry face, leaning over me. Mrs. Dixon was back, brandishing the EpiPen I kept in my purse.

In case she had no clue where to administer the shot, I clumsily reached out the fingers of my left hand, bending my wrist that way as much as the sling would allow, trying to motion to my thigh.

My eyes closed, tears squeezing out.

Bzz.

I tried, once more, a last-ditch effort for air.

But my paralyzed diaphragm refused, my locked-up throat denied me. I was done. My parents would never know what happened to me. Rory would go on and kiss some other girl before me. All of my dreams were done.

Bzz—

A second later, there was a violent punch to my thigh where

Mrs. Dixon jabbed the needle in. My body jerked, automatically reacting to the blow.

But there was no air to cry out with the pain.

Seconds passed. Seconds I didn't have.

The pain from the shot gradually receded as the fist clenching my chest began to loosen.

I gasped my first ragged breath.

Bzzzz.

Another breath came, then another, each marginally less raspy and laborious and painful than the first. I began to hope, to *believe* in the possibility that—for the time being—I would not be dying after all.

My eyes opened.

Mrs. Dixon squatted a few feet away from me, her forehead scrunched up. Was she actually worried about me? She noticed my open eyes and blew out a breath. Relief?

Bzzzzzz.

As I lay there, slowly coming back from my near-death experience, she rolled up a magazine.

I dropped my head to the side. She stalked the bees, slamming the magazine down. I imagined their bodies crushed, innards oozing out. They'd get no sympathy from me.

I set my swollen right hand on my chest, relaxing as it rose up and down, calming more as my breaths grew deeper and stronger.

Mrs. Dixon *should* have been worried. Kidnapping was one thing. But having your kid murder someone? That was something else entirely.

The buzzing finally stopped. She tossed the magazine on the table and walked back over to me.

I wasn't sure if I had the power of speech yet, but I had to try. My voice was soft and shaky, but still audible. "She tried to kill me."

Mrs. Dixon shrugged. The casual gesture implied she couldn't give a crap. But the tightness of her arms to her sides betrayed her. She had been scared, perhaps still was. Yet she tried her best to seem uncaring as she held her chin high. "Well, now I saved you. So that makes us even."

Even? What was she thinking? Even if I had wanted to speak, there were no words.

She pointed. I couldn't see exactly where, but knew exactly what she meant when she said, "And you'd better clean that up or you won't be getting any more food."

Then she walked out and slammed the door.

Click!

That was it? I could have died on her watch, and that was it?

Lacking the power to yell anything after her, I simply raised my red, swollen right hand. As viciously as my zapped, anaphylactically shocked body would allow, I snapped up my middle finger.

6

EXHAUSTED FROM THE ordeal of almost checking out for good, I couldn't do anything but lie there, my right cheek on the green indoor/outdoor carpet. In addition to all my previous aches and pains and bruises, there was a new laundry list of afflictions:

My face was hot and sweaty.

My thigh ached from the EpiPen assault.

I was still not entirely convinced that each breath would not be my last.

My stung hand throbbed and resembled a swollen, misshapen claw.

I remained on the floor, listening to the hubbub upstairs as Mrs. Dixon yelled at Flute Girl.

"What were you thinking? What do you think would happen if she had died? What would we have done then?"

Despite my current state of misery, I managed to smile a bit. The little freak came across as ignorant, but was she? I didn't think so. She knew exactly what she was doing. And exactly what would happen.

The whole thing was planned.

Flute Girl not only had to find a box, but she had to capture the bees and wait until her mom left. So Flute Girl absolutely did know right from wrong. At least, enough to know that her mother would not have approved. A sociopath was conniving and deceitful. A psychopath was sinister and violent. One of the differences was that a psychopath lacked remorse.

Flute Girl definitely had the cunning of one and the pro-active cruelty of the other. Remorse? That would be the true test. I'd have to wait and see if I was dealing with a future monster or just a child who didn't have her moral compass screwed on right.

Mrs. Dixon kept yelling. "What am I supposed to do with you?"

There were certainly some suggestions floating around in my woozy, pissed-off head.

I groaned and managed to sit up. I leaned back against the wall and bent my knees. Carefully, I tucked in my slung-up arm and set my right elbow on my knee, elevating my stung hand as much as the pain would allow. Maybe that would help reduce the swelling.

"Don't you dare go near her again! Understand?"

I found myself slightly comforted by the fact that Mrs. Dixon was at least bothered that I might have died.

So she *didn't* want that to happen. Me neither.

I needed that not to happen.

I had to stay rational, organized. Flute Girl was obviously aware of my allergy, which meant that she had read the back of my MedicAlert bracelet. And Mrs. Dixon knew exactly where my EpiPen was, which meant she had done an inventory of my purse.

Had she spent my money? Used my credit cards?

If my mom or anyone tried to trace my whereabouts, they'd be certain to check that. I hoped she *was* stupid enough to use my cards.

What really gave me the willies was what these two lunatics could find out about me. My journal was in a secret pocket of the custom carry-on that had been in the trunk of my car. If they found it, they would know a lot more about me than anyone else knew, except maybe Rory.

I was so careful about what I revealed to my fans. Bloggers constantly interviewed me for this or that, but I managed to give them enough to keep everyone satisfied without giving them too much. And I blogged myself. Social media was a requirement for authors.

Honestly, when hundreds of people commented on my posts, it was a total ego boost. But there was so much I kept for myself. Rory was the only one I told everything to. Nearly everything.

Part of me was afraid that the readers wouldn't like the real me. I put on a good show, of course: Successful teenage author has the world by the proverbial balls.

If they only knew how insecure I really was about everything *except* writing. Which was why, at first, I didn't tell Rory *quite* everything.

For a long time, he had no idea that he was not only my first boyfriend, but also my first friend. From kindergarten to eighth grade, I'd attended a small charter school that billed itself as unique, different from the local public school. With all the bullying in public schools, it found a publicity niche: a kinder, gentler environment.

What a load of crap.

The first day of kindergarten, I wore black Mary Janes, a black-and-white-striped T-shirt, denim skirt, and perfect lacy black-and-white-striped socks. Mom did my hair in one long braid down my back, almost like a tail. Maybe the braid was the mistake. Or maybe it was the shirt. Most probably the black and white.

I didn't know. How could I? I was five.

I simply wanted everything to be perfect.

Every day when my mom went to work, the last thing she did was walk into a cloud of perfume. So I sneaked into her room, plucked a bottle off the bureau, and spritzed several pumps of perfume in the air, walking through the mist, turning, and walking through again.

"Olivia!" Mom took the perfume out of my hand. "Oh, sweetie." She smiled. "Well, at least you'll smell nice."

So I packed up my new pink book bag with pristine crayons and shiny safety scissors and colored pencils and everything else on the school supply list for East Cascades Charter School. I was breathless with anticipation.

My grandma had always watched me when my parents were at work, so as an only child, I hadn't had a lot of interaction with children, other than some children of my parents' friends. But I had been looking forward to starting school because I was smart, liked learning, and loved to read.

Above all, I desperately wanted a friend. We ran a little late that morning, and I knew there was something I'd forgotten to do as I buckled my seat belt. I told my mom, "I'm going to find a best friend today."

Mom smiled. "I bet you will." When she was a lawyer, she always dressed in smart suits and heels, her dark hair in a perfect bob that required regular trips to the salon to maintain. She had no doubt that I would turn out to be smart and talented and, above all, popular.

At the circle drive at school, I hopped out and ran up to the front door. A sweet gray-haired lady introduced herself as Miss Nola and pointed me to the classroom. The soles of my Mary Janes clicked happily the entire way.

Inside the room, I stopped to take a breath. A piano stood in the corner, an art table ran across the entire back wall, and a glass fish tank sat on top of a short, squat filing cabinet. The room smelled enticing, like Elmer's glue and finger paint.

"Olivia." The voice was musical. Miss Molly was short for a grown-up, with a blunt red bob and freckles sprayed across her nose. To me, she was perfection. Miss Molly opened her arms, and I ran into them. "Welcome, welcome! Can you go over and put your bag in your cubby? Then find a chair in the Happy Time Circle."

I was reluctant to leave Miss Molly's embrace, but I bounced over to the wall across from the windows and found my name, then placed my bag on the hook. I felt a pressure between my legs and realized what I had forgotten.

I wondered if I should ask Miss Molly where to go, but she was surrounded by other children, so I skipped over to the circle of chairs and sat down next to a girl in a pink dress with short, brown hair who smiled at me. Her name tag read SAVANNA. I smiled back as I pinched my legs tightly together.

Another girl, with brown curly hair, red shorts, and a blue T-shirt, name tag bearing CECILLE, sat on the other side of the girl, as a boy sat next to me.

I didn't know very much about boys, and I didn't want to sit by one. He wore a red polo shirt and jeans and what looked like a smaller version of my dad's weekend work boots. His name tag said DONNY.

Donny told me, "You stink."

Savanna said, "That is not nice to say."

Donny leaned closer to me and took a big sniff. He scrunched up his nose. "Well, she does. She stinks."

I said, "It's my mom's perfume."

Cecille stood up and walked over to me. She sniffed and then quickly pinched her nose shut with her fingers. "Oh, she does."

Tears welled up in my eyes.

More children took their seats, all of them staring at Cecille and Donny, who seemed to be suffering greatly in my presence. I'd had enough. "I don't stink!"

"Yes, you do!" said Donny. "You smell just like . . . just like . . . a skunk!"

Cecille giggled. "Yeah, a skunk!"

Savanna in the pink dress shook a finger at her. "That is mean."

A girl started to sit down, but Cecille waved her off. "No! You don't want to sit by a skunk!"

Donny grabbed my braid. "See? She even has a *skunky* tail!"

Tears slipped down my cheeks, and I put my hands over my face, amid the whispers of "Skunk!"

Why didn't Miss Molly come over there and stop them? Why didn't she save me?

Donny pinched my stomach, hard.

And then, I couldn't help it. The pee seeped out and drenched my underwear, turned my denim skirt dark in patches, and then spread to the edges of the chair.

Drip. Drip. Drip onto the primary-colored blocks of carpet that made up the Happy Time Circle. The green square darkened in spots.

"Look!" cried Donny. "The skunk peed her pants! Now she smells like . . . skunk piss!" He pinched his nostrils shut, and the other children followed suit.

I looked to Savanna for help.

Slowly, Savanna slid her chair over, away from me. Then she pinched her nose shut as well.

Miss Molly approached the Happy Time Circle, a dark look on her face. But she said nothing to the children all holding their noses. Instead, Miss Molly rolled her eyes slightly and sighed, mumbling under her breath, "I thought we'd at least make it to recess before someone did that."

The classroom aide was Miss Nola, the gray-haired lady

from earlier. No longer sweet, she scowled and pinched my elbow with old, wrinkled fingers. "Come on."

When I stood up, warm pee dripped down my legs and into my perfect lacy black-and-white socks. By the time we reached the single-stall faculty bathroom at the end of the hall, each footstep squished. The aide opened up a new package of white underwear and handed me one, along with some rough brown paper towels. "Clean yourself up. I'll be out here."

Through sobs and sniffles, I held a paper towel under the water until it was a soaked, mushy ball, then pushed the button of the soap dispenser and let the glittery pink ooze out. I wiped my legs, shivering as the cool water and soap dripped down, and dried them with a scratchy paper towel. Some of the soap dried sticky.

As hard as I tried to clean off the smell, it lingered. Donny was right. I smelled like skunk piss.

I put on the big and baggy underwear, which felt like it might fall down at any moment. That afternoon, after enduring an entire day of children holding their noses whenever they came near me, I trudged out to my mom's car.

She grinned. "Well! Did you pick out a best friend yet?"

Instead of answering her question, I claimed I had a stomachache. When I got home, I ran upstairs and stripped off my clothes, my new Mary Janes, the no-longer-perfect lacy black-and-white socks, and stuffed them all in the garbage.

I was five years old. Old enough to know I had not turned out to be the child my mom wanted me to be. Old enough to know I was already a failure at life.

7

STILL TOO TIRED to move, all my efforts were focused on breathing regularly. I sat there on the floor, staring at the concrete wall on the other side of the room. I hadn't reminisced about my school years for a while. In my day-to-day life, there was no time to think. There was definitely no time to wallow in the past.

I was doing what I liked, getting paid a lot of money for it, and was about to head off to college. I hadn't ever planned to tell Rory much about my torturous grade-school years. And why the hell would I? They were bad enough to live through once.

I had been afraid to tell him. Who would ever want to love someone who had been known as Skunk Piss for much of her childhood?

Maybe Miss Molly was blind, I don't know, but she never stopped them from tormenting me. Maybe she didn't want to deal with it. Maybe she was stupid. Maybe she'd been bullied in childhood and was relieved that no one bothered her.

I didn't tell my mom that year. Or the next. Not that she

was absent from my life, or even school. She brought cup-cakes for every open house. I liked those nights. Both my parents, holding my hands, lingering over my desk to see my latest drawing or math or writing. On those nights, I was like everyone else, simply another kid with proud parents.

Telling them the truth would have ruined it.

Their pride kept me silent. Because I loved that they were proud of me. And seeing what I was really like in the classroom on a daily basis—weak, victimized, cowering alone at recess, sitting at the end of the lunch table by myself—would have deflated them. Maybe they would have felt like they failed. The biggest reason I never told them?

I was terrified they wouldn't love me anymore.

No one wants to be the parent of the class loser.

Their love and pride were all I had to hold on to, and all it took to keep me silent.

Finally, in fifth grade, I'd had enough.

Why did it take so long? Really, it wasn't like I was walking up to other little girls and asking them to jump rope or share my Nutella at snack time, then having to deal with their saying no. I interacted with none of them, so there was little chance for any actual rejection to occur.

Plus, there was the little matter of the pariah cloud over my head.

But children are optimistic at heart. So I waited for someone to ask me to play. And in the meantime, I kept busy.

I read. Constantly. From second grade on, the librarian would let me stay in at recess and help her shelve books. I loved being there in the quiet windowless room, alone with all the shelves stuffed with stories, many happier than mine, but some much more tragic. Those books were my friends.

Charlie Bucket and Lucy Pevensie and Harry Potter. They begged me to read them. So I was okay as long as I had books. Maybe, deep inside, I held out hope that I could escape like Charlie and Lucy and Harry had. Like one day I would be swept away to run a chocolate factory or discover I had secret magic skills. Or maybe I would find a wardrobe and say, "Screw this, I'm going to Narnia."

In fifth grade, our teacher was mean. We'd had Miss Reed as a long-term sub in fourth grade when our teacher had a baby, and she had been kind and patient. Even to me. But when she returned in the fall as Mrs. Klein, she apparently took her new full-time job seriously. Maybe it was Mrs. Klein's constantly demanding so much of the entire class. But for whatever reason, it seemed like nobody had energy left after dealing with her to mess with me. At least some of the time. Sure, there were days when I was treated like a leper, nothing new. But there were also days when the girls who had tormented me for years were, if not exactly my friends, at least my allies.

The enemy of my enemy is my friend. Something on that order.

Some days, it was as if they realized we needed each other to survive fifth grade.

And I began to trust. Cecille had blossomed into a lovely-looking ten-year-old. Still mean as hell on the inside, which just goes to show you can't exactly judge a book by its cover. But even she had mellowed with the advent of Mrs. Klein's fascist regime. At lunch there were even some days when I sat with her and her friends, who actually seemed like they were my friends, too.

And why wouldn't they want to be my friends?

Despite my enduring nickname, which had been shortened to Skunky, I did not smell. My parents had money. I always had the best shampoos and soaps and perfumes and trendiest jeans and dresses and shoes. I got good grades. I wasn't terrific in gym class, but I wasn't ever picked last, either. And slowly, I began to let down the walls that had bricked their way up around me since that first day of kindergarten.

Then, in March, a new girl showed up. Christine had flaming red hair and freckles all over her face. She was pretty and wore white jeans with a blue sweater. That first day, cheeseburger and fries day, I took my tray in the cafeteria and stopped as I decided where to sit.

The new girl sat by herself at the end of the lunch table. But instead of bowing her head low over her tray, trying to seem invisible like I usually did when I ate alone, she held her head high, looking around at everyone.

Christine seemed fearless.

I wanted to sit by her. Christine knew nothing about me, none of my history. Finally, I could have a friend. Perhaps even a best friend. I hadn't been invited to sit with Cecille and her crew that day, so I took one step toward Christine.

Cecille stepped in front of me. "Skunky, you sitting with us?"

I glanced quickly over at Christine and swallowed. For a matter of seconds I considered my options because there usually were none. *Maybe I will blow off Cecille, blow her off like she doesn't matter, and go claim Christine as my one and only friend.* Instead, believing that things had changed, *hoping* that at last I was truly part of the powerful faction of the fifth grade, I nodded.

We sat down. I dumped a packet of ketchup onto my plate and dipped a crinkled fry into it.

Cecille leaned forward toward the center of the table, beckoning us in with a hand. Her gaze darted about, conspiratorially. "So, Olivia."

I froze and stopped chewing.

She never—none of them ever—called me anything but Skunky. If there was a teacher or other adult around, they refrained from calling me anything.

Cecille continued, "We've been talking."

I swallowed, waiting. "Yeah?"

She raised and lowered a shoulder. "We'd like you to be a permanent member at our lunch table." She looked around at the others. "Right?"

The rest nodded, some *um-hmm*ing, some giggling as they ate their cheeseburgers.

I was too stunned to say anything. It had finally happened. All those years of torment were over. Had they realized I wasn't going to cave? I wasn't going to go begging them to be my friends? Was that what they'd been waiting for all this time? And they finally decided it was time to reward me by letting me in?

Whatever the reason, I didn't care. I smiled and nodded.

"There's one thing you have to do," she said.

I leaned in as Cecille whispered in my ear. My stomach clenched as she told me the price of being included and slipped something onto my tray.

Later, back in class, I told myself, *You don't have to do it. You can turn them down. Becoming one of them is not worth it.*

But instead, I closed my fist around the item in my hand and took my seat, waiting for the right moment. We were in creative writing, my favorite part of the day. Because not only did I like reading to escape my world, I also liked writing my own worlds. I bent my head over my desk and began working.

"Pssst."

I looked up. Mrs. Klein's seating chart put the trouble-making boys in the front row, good students in the back, which left me in the second-to-last row. Cecille was across the aisle and one seat back from me. She jabbed a finger at Christine's empty seat, which was right behind mine. Up at the front of the room, Christine was sharpening a pencil. Mrs. Klein entered grades in her computer, her back to us.

I glanced over at Cecille. She glared at me and mouthed, *Do it.*

I opened my left hand. A white packet of ketchup lay there,

a little scrunched from where I'd been squeezing it. I quickly ripped the corner open and looked back up at the front.

Christine still hunched over the sharpener; Mrs. Klein still faced the other way. I grabbed a tissue out of my desk, crumpled it, then stood up and walked to the garbage can at the back of the room, tossing it in. On my way back, I dropped the open packet of ketchup on Christine's chair, then quickly took my own seat.

She began to head back toward me. *Please, let her see it, let her see it. Don't let her sit on it.*

And I realized there was no way Christine could miss it. She was coming from the front; she would totally look before she sat down. I breathed a sigh of relief. She would pick it up, throw it away, wonder who had done it.

But nothing bad would have happened. Nothing that I couldn't take back.

"Pssst!"

I whipped my head toward Cecille.

A big smile on her face, she waved at Christine. Christine hesitated for a second, and then a smile spread across her face. She waved back. She wasn't looking at her seat. The new girl was simply responding to a friendly classmate.

Christine sat down. Apparently without looking, because she quickly jumped to her feet behind me. "What is on my—" The butt of her white jeans was splotched bright red.

"Oh no," said Cecille, so loud that everyone turned around. "Did you get your period, Christine?"

Christine's hip brushed my arm as she ran for the door at the front of the room.

Mrs. Klein looked up. "You need a pass, young lady!"

But Christine was gone. And the entire class was laughing. Well, the entire class except for me. I sat there and tried to persuade myself not to cry.

And all these years later, sitting in the basement, I hated Cecille for making me feel like I had to do that. And I still wished I could take it back.

8

I TRIED TO stand, and actually managed to get up on my knees. But I had to bend forward and rest on my right elbow to keep from passing out. Slowly, I straightened up. My vision swam.

I took a couple of deep breaths until it cleared. "Maybe I'll just stay here for a bit." I leaned back against the wall and slid down on my butt, my knees bent.

I shut my eyes.

A door slammed overhead. An engine started. Tires crunching gravel.

I opened my eyes. Had Mrs. Dixon left again? *Seriously?*

I hoped she took her demon child with her.

The floor above my head creaked.

I froze.

Flute Girl was still in the house.

I exhaled. "I hope to hell your mother put the fear of God into you." I didn't know what I'd do if she tried anything. There had been only one EpiPen in my purse. So if Flute Girl decided to try the let's-see-what-happens-when-the-allergic-girl-gets-stung game again, I'd be toast.

Steps on the stairs. Quiet, like she was trying to be sneaky, but she sucked at that part. Flute Girl was more skilled at confronting people with a stick in her hand.

"Get the hell out of here!" I yelled. "Just leave me alone."

No response.

I wished I could get up and go bang on the door, but I was still working on breathing. Then a sound started. A low note on her flute. Then another. A song. She was playing a freaking song.

Nuh nah, nuh nah nuh nah na naa naa, nah nuh nah nuh naa naa . . .

Was that . . . ?

"Holy crap."

Lady Gaga.

Flute Girl nailed it. If I didn't hate her guts, I might have been impressed.

Hopefully, Mrs. Dixon had hidden the key to the padlock, maybe even taken it with her. So Flute Girl had been forced to shift from killing me with bees to serenading me with a pop music medley.

She moved on to "All the Single Ladies," then some old Maroon 5. I said nothing as she played and gave no indication that I even heard her. But as song segued into song segued into song, I began to wonder if she was still trying to kill me, only in a different way.

I got to my feet and slowly made my way over to the bed. I

went the long way to avoid the shards of china and spaghetti mess on the floor and collapsed on the bed, wincing as the bounce jarred my bad shoulder and my throbbing hand. I awkwardly scooted up and laid my head on the pillow, then pulled the blanket over my head. It drowned out a bit of the music, but not entirely.

I groaned and patted the blanket closer in around my ears. But then it was too close to my face. After my brush with never breathing again, I couldn't take it and pushed it away.

The ceiling was made up of white tiles. Clean, though, no mold.

The demonic flutist's repertoire moved on to what could have been either Rihanna or an abysmal rendition of a Coldplay hit. Unsure, I tried to think of something to get my mind off the noise.

Unintentionally, my mind went back to fifth grade, to that day.

CHRISTINE RAN OUT OF THE ROOM. I SAT THERE, NOT LAUGHING with everyone else, feeling remorse for what I'd done. For what Cecille had made me do. Sure, I had a choice. But did I really?

What if I had said no? Cecille and her group would have barred me for good. But by completing the task, I had a shot at being embraced by her group. Because I had always been someone who looked at the big picture.

After about half an hour, Christine came back into the room wearing some baggy gray sweatpants, balled-up white jeans in one hand. I stared down at my math book as she neared me.

I was anxious for afternoon recess. I wanted to talk to Cecille and the others. I'd done what they said, which made me part of them now.

But Mrs. Klein was furious at the disruption and put us on lockdown until the end of the day. No recess. No talking. And after school, my mom was waiting outside, so I couldn't do anything more than go straight to the car.

At school the next day, I took my seat. I tried to get Cecille's attention, but her back was to me as she talked to a girl across the aisle. I turned and glanced sideways at Christine, whose gaze was trained out the window. She had on black leggings and a cream-colored sweater. No chance of repeating the humiliation of the day before with dark pants, I supposed.

Art was the first class of the day. But instead, Mrs. Klein said, "I've informed Mr. Millis that you'll be a little late to art today." Someone groaned. Mrs. Klein glared and crossed her arms. "I have a little story for you all."

"Once upon a time, there were five buffaloes. They decided they wanted to go roller skating. Now four of the buffaloes took off, leaving the other buffalo behind. She wasn't very good at roller skating, so they laughed at her and left her behind because she was so slow."

Someone coughed.

Mrs. Klein continued. "The buffalo sat there, alone. And she began to cry because the other buffaloes were mean to her."

I slipped down a little in my seat. Where was she going with that? Because it seemed to me like, more often than not, I was the buffalo left alone. Was she finally going to address the bullying in the room?

"Finally, one of the buffaloes noticed the other one, crying all by herself, and went back to help her up. She joined the other buffaloes, and they all roller-skated together after that."

Um, what? I scratched my head.

Mrs. Klein uncrossed her arms and shook a finger at us. "It has come to my attention that there has been some bad behavior in this room. We have a new girl, and I will not tolerate anyone treating her any way but the way we should treat others. Nicely."

My face began to burn. *Seriously? I get treated like crap for years, and now the new girl gets picked on one day and gets a protective lecture from the teacher?*

Mrs. Klein scowled. "Mostly, I'm incredibly disappointed that the one person who knows what it's like to be picked on, the one person who should know better—" Her gaze turned to me. As did several heads of others in the room.

I slunk further down in my seat, and my face got even hotter.

"—was involved in this. So this behavior will stop. You will all get along with one another from now on. Do I make myself clear?"

I nodded, and everyone I could see also nodded. They wanted the lecture to be over. She dismissed us for art class, and we walked, single file, out in the hallway.

We sat where we wanted in the art room, on long benches at cafeteria-style tables. Cecille sat down, and I headed for that table. But when I got there, she set a hand on the bench beside her. "You're not sitting here, Skunky."

I froze. My heart began to pound. My hands trembled at my sides. Was she messing with me? I had done what she asked! Risked getting in trouble for it. She had to be joking.

But the girls around her sported smug looks and shook their heads. One pinched her nose. Cecille looked behind me and called out, "Christine, come sit with us."

I turned and almost bumped into Christine. The new girl glared at me. "Cecille told me what you did. What did I ever do to you, Skunky?" She sat down next to Cecille, in the spot that was supposed to be mine.

Cecille grinned at me. "Go sit somewhere else."

Blinking back sudden stinging tears, I quickly went to a table at the other side of the room. There, I slid in beside a couple of girls who wouldn't care if I was there or not. They would ignore me, like everyone else did, but at least they wouldn't say anything mean to me.

I stared down at the table, trying to keep the tears from progressing. And I reached up to the back of my neck and rubbed. *Don't cry. Don't cry.*

My fingers got tangled in the hair at the back of my neck, and I yanked. The resulting sting made me jump. But the shock also, momentarily, took away the urge to cry. I reached up again and snapped out another hair. Slowly, after a few more, I was calm. I wasn't going to cry. I had control.

What's the saying? You spend your entire adulthood trying to recover from your childhood?

I didn't know if that was true, but some days it seemed like it made sense.

The hair pulling began that day in fifth grade and got worse over the summer. By fall I had a bald patch on the back right side of my head. I could disguise it because my hair was long, so I wore a side braid every day of sixth grade. Seventh grade I changed it to a braid going back into a ponytail, and eighth grade I gave up and wore a thick headband. At least I could change the colors to match my outfits.

One summer day right after eighth grade ended, my mom and I were shopping. I was in the dressing room at American Eagle, trying to fit into a pair of size six shorts, which I knew was never going to happen. Along with the hair pulling, I'd also taken to snacking away my stress and loneliness.

"Olivia, are they on yet?"

"Just a sec." I held my breath, squeezed in my gut, and buttoned the shorts. Then I pulled off my tank top to try on a shirt. But my headband got caught in the strap, and I yanked it off. Just then, my mom reached the end of her patience and pushed open the door.

"Sweetie, I'd like to get home by . . ." She trailed off as her mouth fell open. Then her eyes narrowed and she touched the side of my head. "What happened? My God, you've got a bald patch!"

"Get out!" I shoved her away, trying to close the door on her. "Get out! *Please*, get out!"

But she pushed her way back in and shut the door behind her. We were inches away. Clutching the tank top to my chest with one hand, I tried to fix my hair with the other.

"Have you been doing that to yourself?"

My chin wobbled and my eyes filled with tears. I shut them, hoping to avert the flow. I nodded.

"But why? Why would you do that? Is something wrong?"

After years of hiding, years of keeping secret that I continued to be the most reviled kid in my class, I opened my eyes and the tears spilled out.

Mom pulled me to her. She stroked my hair, long and slow. Her words were soft. "Tell me. You can tell me."

My mouth was mashed into the shoulder of her white T-shirt, so my words were rather mumbled. "Kids pick on me."

"What?" She stopped stroking for a moment, and then began again. "Why? Why would they do that?"

Oh God. How many times had I asked myself that?

I swallowed and took a shuddery breath. Then I lifted my head over her shoulder and stared at myself in the mirror on the door. My eyes were red, my face was blotchy, hair everywhere. And I told her the truth, starting with the first day of kindergarten.

Her shoulders slumped. "Why didn't you ever say anything?"

"Why didn't you ever notice?"

Her face crumpled, and she set a hand over her eyes and began to cry.

Instantly, I regretted my words.

"I don't know. I don't know!" She dropped her hand. Her mascara was running as she put her hands on either side of my face. "It's my work. I'm quitting tomorrow."

"No, Mom, come on." I set a hand on her shoulder. "You love being a lawyer."

She shook her head. "I was too busy with my career to notice my child was being bullied to the point of . . ." She trailed off. Then she leaned forward and kissed my bald patch. "I'm done. I'm quitting."

"You don't have to quit. But please don't make me go back there."

She raised her eyebrows. "Are you kidding me? You're never stepping foot in that school again."

Later, when we needed to explain home school for my official book biography, we chalked it up to my busy writing schedule. And after I had stated it so many times in interviews, that pragmatic falsehood became in my mind the real reason for spending my high school years in the comfort of my own home.

But that was a load of crap.

My official bio also left out my therapy. Turns out my behavior had a name. Trichotillomania. It took a few months of pills and sessions, but I stopped. Journaling about the years of bullying was part of my therapy. And when I finally broke down and spilled everything to Rory, I felt like a load had been lifted. Because he knew everything and still wanted to be with me.

Success had been the best revenge. I was out on book tour, staying in five-star hotels and having strangers stand for hours in line to see me, while Cecille and her posse were sitting in stupid school. And yeah, I did some stalking online. I had a book deal and would be going to a huge university. Cecille was going to community college to be a dental assistant.

One day maybe she'd clean my teeth.

So I was over those years, pretty much. But I didn't quit writing about them in my journal, in the trunk of my car. The one I did not want Flute Girl's mother to get her hands on. Because in those hands, as long as I was her prisoner in that basement, my journal had the potential to be just as destructive to me as a box full of bees.

9

FLUTE GIRL FINALLY ran out of breath and clomped up the stairs far louder than she'd descended. Obviously, there wasn't anyone there to sneak up on. I shut my eyes and managed to doze. When I woke, I felt a little better. I rolled over on my side and stared down at the spaghetti and broken shards of china. I'd have to be careful or I'd end up cutting myself and—

I blinked.

Stupid.

I'd been worried about finding a weapon, and there was an entire pile of sharp objects. Some were too tiny; I wouldn't have been able to pick them up without cutting myself. But some were larger. Those could definitely do some damage.

I stood and walked around the bed. I chose a jagged piece the size of my palm. A pink flower lay nearly in the middle of it, as did a stain of spaghetti sauce. I picked out another piece of the flower part for good measure. And then, another. I walked back around the bed and slipped them under the pillow. Then I went to the bathroom and brought out the flimsy wastebasket.

I didn't really want to clean up the mess. But it might mean a better chance of Mrs. Dixon not noticing that any of the pieces were missing.

The crunch of tires on gravel. A car door slammed.

"Crap." Quickly, I reached for the debris.

Footsteps on the stairs signaled that I was nearly out of time.

Click!

The door flew open.

Mrs. Dixon stood there, in the same flowered smock, scrub pants, and shiny red clogs as before. "You're cleaning?"

I nodded and tried my best to look like I wasn't rushing to get done. But my heart pounded. A bead of sweat slipped down my temple.

She came toward me.

I froze, then straightened up and backed away from her. She held out her hands. "Here, you're making more of a mess. I'll do it."

When I didn't move, she took the wastebasket from me. I glanced down at the mess and walked around her, sitting on the other side of the bed as she cleaned. She said, "You seem to have recovered." But her tone was almost snide, like she thought I had been faking.

"I took a nap."

She paused and locked her eyes with mine. "Must be nice, to take a nap when you feel like it."

My right hand clenched into a fist. "There's not a lot else to do in here."

She tilted her head. "I imagine when you're home, you have the luxury to do whatever the hell you want, whenever the hell you want to do it."

She was pissing me off. Was it on purpose?

Mrs. Dixon kept talking. "That must be nice. You didn't even have to go to high school, did you?" Obviously, she knew the answer already or she wouldn't have brought it up. Was she trying to make me sound like some kind of pampered, spoiled teenager who had always had everything handed to her?

Because sure, maybe it seemed like that on the outside. Maybe the damn *bio* on the back of my books made it seem that way, but I had been through a ton of lousy years before anything got better. The past few years *had* been pretty sweet, though. I loved having a nice car and being able to buy pretty much anything I wanted and choosing what I wanted to do every day. I wasn't ashamed to admit that I relished going to conventions or conferences or book signings and having people fight to talk to me, get near me. Finally, I was the girl at the lunch table whom everyone wanted to sit by.

No one was going to make me feel bad about my success. No one. The universe owed me, and no one would get me to think differently. Especially not Mrs. Daryl Dixon.

I realized my face had grown hot, and my heart was pounding.

She bent back over, pushing the mess into the wastebasket. The back of her neck was exposed. Soft. Pale.

Vulnerable.

I gulped.

Those sharp pieces of broken plate hidden beneath the pillow could do some damage to that patch of flesh.

My hand slid under the pillow.

My fingers closed around a jagged piece of china. I quickly flipped it around so that I held the smooth side. Then I slowly got up on the bed, rising to my knees.

"You have no idea how lucky you have it, do you?"

Just keep talking.

Gingerly, not to mention painfully, I made my way across the bed.

Slide right hand. Right knee. Left knee.

Breathe.

"I try and teach my own daughter to be honest and work hard and good things will happen. She works so hard at her flute."

Slide right hand. Right knee. Left knee.

Breathe.

"That should be enough in this country. Work hard. Do all the right things. Everything should be okay." She sighed. "But I don't want her to turn out like me. Working at a nursing home. Giving sponge baths to old people who can't even remember my name from day to day."

Slide right hand—

I leaned forward too fast and lost my balance, falling forward onto my right elbow. The mattress jiggled. I stifled a gasp and scrunched my eyes shut.

Please please please . . .

"I had a dream. I had a dream, and it was taken away. I don't want that to happen to her."

I slowly let out my breath and opened my eyes.

She was still cleaning up, oblivious to me.

Right knee. Left knee.

Breathe.

I paused, gazing down at that patch of pale skin. Then I lowered myself until I knelt on the edge of the bed, my weight distributed so that I was balanced solidly.

I leaned over and raised my good arm, poised above her.

One good jab, that's all it would take.

I didn't have to kill her, only create enough pain to startle her, distract her enough to be able to get out the door and lock it. Then I'd deal with Flute Girl.

"Because sometimes all the hard work and honesty in the world doesn't mean a damn thing if someone else is dishonest and uses . . ."

I shut out her babble and licked my lips. *Just one good jab.*

I swallowed and tightened my grip.

You can do this.

My heart raced. I steeled myself, poised to pounce—

"MAMA!" Flute Girl stood in the doorway, eyes wide, arm thrust out, pointing at me.

I lost my balance and fell forward.

Before I went even a foot, Mrs. Dixon grabbed my wrist and

yanked me all the way off the bed. I slammed face-first onto the floor.

The breath was knocked out of me, and a fresh bolt of pain shot through my shoulder. I hung on tight to that jagged piece of plate.

To no avail. Mrs. Dixon was on my back, pinning me to the floor. She put a hand on my head and smashed one side of my face into the bits of plate and spaghetti sauce smeared on the floor. Her knee crushed my wrist, and I couldn't hold on anymore. My fingers opened. I let the weapon go.

Her knee lifted, and I tried to lash out with my good arm.

Something immediately pinned it down. Something warm and squirming and alive. Flute Girl was sitting on my arm. I couldn't use my slung-up arm to move myself. I could only lie there, panting, my heart pounding so hard it drummed in my ears.

Mrs. Dixon left for a second. There was a rustle of bed-covers. Then her legs came into view.

"You had quite a stash."

Clink.

A piece of the broken plate landed in the wastebasket.

Clink.

Another.

Then her weight was back on top of me. The two of them had me immobilized. My shoulder was on fire, and my cheek stung where broken bits of the plate dug into it.

Mrs. Dixon's breath on my ear was hot and moist. "Did you really think I'd let you hurt me or my daughter?"

I said nothing.

Flute Girl piped up, "She could have killed you."

Mrs. Dixon grabbed my hair and pulled up my head. She slammed it down again, my forehead hitting the green indoor/outdoor carpet—and the cement it barely cushioned—like a sledgehammer.

I moaned at the thick surge of pain.

Her mouth was back at my ear. "How would you feel? How would you feel if someone tried to hurt you?"

"Just kill me already." A mumble only. I wanted to yell the words, wanted to scream them. But my head was splitting apart, and it was all I could do to talk. "You've been trying to kill me since you found me on the road."

I braced myself for another head slam. Instead, her hold on me loosened for a moment. Actually, so long a moment that I considered trying to shove Flute Girl off my arm and make a break for it. But then her weight was back on top of me. "I'm sick of listening to you talk," said Mrs. Dixon.

Good. I shut my eyes. *Maybe she'll leave.*

Something brushed against my forehead, and I opened my eyes. A pink washcloth with orange polka dots dangled in front of me.

What the hell?

With strong, cruel fingers, she pinched my cheeks so my mouth opened. I tried to keep my lips glued together. But she pried them open and stuffed the washcloth in my mouth.

"No!" But the word was a grunt as the cloth filled my mouth. I gagged. I wanted to scream.

Breathe through your nose, breathe through your nose.

"There. Now maybe you'll listen."

Calm down, calm down. She just wants to talk.

Something smooth, cool, and hard slid down my cheek. Back up, then down. Languorously. Almost . . . seductively.

The breaths coming out of my nose whistled.

"Isn't it funny, that one side of this is so smooth? Harmless. I could do this all day and nothing would happen to you." The object kept stroking up and down my cheek.

"But the other side . . ."

The coolness was no longer on my cheek.

And then she held the third jagged piece of china in front of my eyes.

I whimpered.

And then the piece disappeared.

". . . is so sharp." The edge poked at my cheek.

I gasped, only there was no air to breathe in my mouth, so it was just a rapid inhale through my nostrils. Again I gagged, then struggled and tried to move, but they had me.

Slowly, the edge trailed down my cheek and back up.

"Imagine trying to do an author photo with a nice long scar." She ran the edge back up and down.

A chill ran down my neck, and goose bumps rose on my arms.

Please don't.

"Maybe we should carve up this whole face."

Tears began to spill over. *Don't. Don't.*

She ran the edge up and down my face. "Don't worry; you could still write, couldn't you? Because God forbid you wouldn't be able to give the world any more of your *fabulous* novels. I mean, you worked so hard on them."

My strangled sobs were quiet groans, stuck in my throat.

Mrs. Dixon pushed the edge into my cheek. "Should we start here?" She pushed, breaking the skin.

An involuntary rush of warmth spread between my legs.

Flute Girl was off me in an instant. "Mama, she peed herself!"

"Oh, balls!" Mrs. Dixon got off me, too, and stood beside Flute Girl. They stared down at me. I could imagine what they saw: a sobbing lump with a washcloth sticking out of my mouth, my face in the spaghetti mess, my leggings darkening as they soaked through.

Mrs. Dixon shook her head and dropped the last piece of broken plate on the rest of the pile.

Clink.

She grabbed one of my feet and dragged me a few feet away from the mess. She quickly placed the remains into the wastebasket, no doubt making sure she'd taken every sharp piece out of my reach. They took the wastebasket and left without another word.

Click!

I ripped the washcloth out of my mouth and freed my sobs. I lay there and cried for my failed escape, for how they could hurt me like that and I could do nothing about it.

They'd managed to turn me into someone I thought I'd left behind.

I was Skunk Piss, once again.

My hand slipped up to my scalp and began to pull. And slowly, hair by stinging hair, I began to feel a little better.

10

I LAY ON the floor until my sobs quieted. I lay there until the pounding kettledrum in my head throttled down to a tom-tom. I lay there until the light outside the window slowly faded. And then, only then—when I was in danger of being in that basement in total darkness—did I finally drag myself to my feet to turn on the bedside lamp.

I sat on the edge of the bed.

My leggings had dried stiff. The sweet, cloying scent of pee hit my nostrils. Half my hair was out of my braids; some strands clumped together with spaghetti sauce hung in front of my eyes. My bare feet were filthy. So many places on my body hurt that I couldn't even differentiate them all.

My stomach growled, reminding me to add starving to the list of things that currently sucked.

The covers were messed up a little, but they were there. As were the pillows. So my one luxury, the nice-smelling bedding, remained. Still mine. I wanted to lie down and sleep, sleep forever. But if I did that, the covers would be ruined. Because I was filthy.

And pissed off. At them, for doing that to me.

But also at myself.

If I had been quicker and struck her instead of hesitating so long, I might have been free. I'd broken my own rule. I'd wasted my only chance of escape early on, the same as all those idiots in horror movies. I had become one of them. A victim. Too weak to hurt her captor when given the opportunity.

"No." I shook my head. No wallowing. That wasn't who I was. Not anymore.

I shuffled to the bathroom, switched on the light, and shut the door. I stepped in front of the sink but didn't look in the mirror. The thought of seeing myself a victim again would put me up against the edge—an edge I didn't dare get any closer to if I had any hope of keeping my wits and getting out alive.

I turned on the cold water, stuck my head under the tap, and drank. Cupping my right hand, I splashed my face. I sucked in a breath. The cold water on all the little cuts stung at first, but then numbed them a bit. I pushed down my underwear and leggings, until they bunched around my ankles, and stepped out of them. I plucked them up with my forefinger and thumb, and then dumped them in the sink.

I turned the other knob and waited until the water ran hot, then pumped several squirts of the lime coconut hand soap into it. The suds grew.

When the sink was nearly full, I turned off the tap and pushed my right hand into the water, which was plenty hot but not scalding. In fact, the warmth seeped into my skin and deeper, comforting me. I started to knead my clothes. Scrubbing with one hand didn't work very well, but I did what I could. The pleasant aroma of lime and coconut brought my senses into focus. I let the clothes soak and turned to open the small cupboard. Pink hand towels and washcloths with orange polka dots lay in tidy stacks. I yanked out a washcloth, stuck it under the tap, and pumped some soap onto it. I washed my lower half, hoping the hand soap—clearly not meant for more sensitive areas—wouldn't give me a rash.

I scrubbed and scrubbed, like I was washing off not only the pee and the dirt from the past two days, but also the memories of those awful years.

I used a towel to dry myself.

I slowly wriggled my sweater off my bad shoulder and dropped it on the floor. I rinsed the washcloth and then ran it under my arms and over my face, and then stopped to look in the mirror. My loose hair stuck up and out, like I'd had a fright and my hair was still reacting. My face was clean at last, but there were abrasions on the right side. On the left, a red scratch ran from my temple to my jaw. Where she'd broken the skin was a streak of dried blood I'd missed.

I unwound the elastics on the ends of my braids and set them on the edge of the sink, then took out what was left of my braids and finger combed my hair. I hit a snag and winced. But there was no comfort in that. Not like there had been earlier.

I growled and smacked the mirror with my palm. Again.

Again and again, until my hand stung. They had driven me back to the hair pulling. I hated them for doing that to me. Pushing me that far.

I took a deep breath. That wouldn't happen again. I wouldn't let them.

After a few minutes and a couple more snags, my hair was finally smooth and free of snarls. It was dirty and greasy as hell, but at least no longer a raging mishmash of ick.

I let the water out of the sink and pushed down on my clothes, trying to get the soap out. I had to run the water a long time before the suds dissipated. Then I wrung the leggings as well as one hand would allow. I hung them on the empty towel rack, then squeezed the underwear in my hand and hung it up, too.

I ran the water again and put my head under the flow, then pumped some of the hand soap onto my head. No telling what the stuff would do to my hair, but the smell itself made me feel better. I rinsed, then stood up and rubbed my hair with a hand towel. After another finger combing, the wet strands hung down, chilly on my bare shoulders.

I wanted to take my grungy white camisole off and wash it, too, but I couldn't be totally naked in there. I wouldn't. I remade my sling, then walked back out to the bed and climbed in. I turned off the bedside lamp. The bathroom bulb still glowed. A little light was reassuring. I lay my head down on the pillow and shut my eyes.

Tomorrow. Tomorrow someone would find my car. They

would find my car and my mom and dad would come to get me. Or Billy. Or Rory.

Someone would come.

My stomach growled.

More water would fill up my belly, lessen the hunger. But I was tired, far too tired to move again. *Please, just let me sleep.*

I drifted off.

A whine woke me up. A screeching, metallic whine that sent chills down my neck.

I sat up. The sound was outside so I looked up at the window. Light beamed in, but not from the sun. It was still night.

The whine stopped and was soon replaced by a rough, idling motor, like a chain saw. Then the whine again, then the motor. The back and forth seemed to go on forever, until the sounds stopped.

Then an engine started up, a loud, rickety machine that gunned and popped, growing louder as it neared my window.

I made my way off the bed to stand under the window, wearing only my sling and camisole.

The bright yard light illuminated the area near the window. The front wheel of a tractor appeared and crept past, revealing a glimpse of the green body, and then the back wheel of the tractor filled the window.

I stepped back a bit, so I could see more. The tractor continued on by, a large chain hanging off the back, pulled taut by whatever it dragged behind. A chunk of red metal appeared in the window, and the tractor stopped, idled a bit, and then suddenly was silent.

I awkwardly clambered on top of the bed, cringing as the bouncing jostled my shoulder. I grabbed the headboard and stood up, making my head nearly level with the glass. My hand gripped the edge of the wooden window frame, and I rose to my tiptoes, precariously balanced as I peered outside.

My view of the object chained to the tractor could not have been more perfect.

My mouth dropped open.

The front half of my beloved Audi was sheared off right past the front seat. They'd cut it up. They'd cut up my car.

Instantly, tears blurred my vision.

My car was no longer on the side of the road. My car was here, sliced into pieces, and dragged into the yard of wherever I was. A wail rose up from inside me and turned into a sob when it hit the air.

No one was ever going to find my car. No one was ever going to find me.

I was so screwed.

"No!" A yell through my tears. I wiped my eyes and peered out the window again.

Like someone watching a train wreck, I couldn't tear myself away from the window. The tractor stayed there, unmoving, that ugly chunk of my car attached to it by the chain.

Was it stuck? Could she not drive it anymore?

Because who else would be driving but Mrs. Dixon? I hadn't

heard anyone in the house besides her and Flute Girl. And she struck me as the independent type—apparently capable of running her own freaking chop shop—someone who would be able to drive her own tractor, have her own farm. Or something.

I shuddered a raspy sob and turned away from the glass.

None of my suspicions boded well for me.

A woman who ran her own farm would probably be self-sufficient, which meant there weren't a lot of visitors. And visitors, particularly unexpected ones, were probably my only hope.

I couldn't keep myself from peering out the window again.

Why had she stopped it there? Was it to show me what she had done? That my car belonged to her, that she could chop it up into little pieces and hide it? Keep anyone from finding it? Or me?

I tried to raise myself higher so I could see farther out.

A face filled the window.

I screamed and lost my grip on the frame. I fell back on the bed and landed faceup, practically spread eagle. The pain in my shoulder swarmed my brain as I stared up at the window and blinked back the tears still clouding my eyes.

A man, no, a boy. My age, maybe a little older. With large dark eyes that leered in at me. The pain subsided slightly. Only then did I remember that I was nude from the waist down.

I gasped and desperately felt around for the blanket. Finally, my fingers found it. I yanked it over my lower half, covering my nakedness. My eyes snapped back up to the window.

He was still there, his face nearly filling the rectangle.

Had he seen me?

No, it was too dark, too dark. He didn't see me. He didn't see me. He didn't—

A slow smile spread across his face. There was a gap between his two front teeth. Then he leaned forward and licked the window, his large pink tongue pressed flat and wide on the dirty glass.

Pulling the blanket with me, I rolled off the bed and ran into the bathroom, fresh tears bursting at the pain the sudden movement caused in my shoulder. With a trembling hand, I switched off the light.

I trembled, my breaths loud in the small, quiet space.

I leaned out into the dark room. His silhouette was still there, his features invisible. In the darkened basement, I had to also be invisible to him.

Small comfort.

I stepped back into the bathroom.

Who was he? He had to have known I was down there. Otherwise, why bother to look in?

My heart still racing, I leaned back out.

The window was empty.

The breath I was holding slowly escaped.

Back in the bathroom, I shut the door and slid my back down it until I was sitting. I pulled the blanket up over me. Now I didn't even have the luxury of a comfortable bed.

No way was I going back out there where he could see me.
Watch me.

So I leaned my head back against the door, shut my eyes,
and prayed for daylight. Everything would be better in the
morning. Because there was certainly no way that things
could get worse.

11

FINALLY, AT SOME point, I drifted off. I didn't dream. When I woke, my body was stiff from sitting on the floor all night. I slowly got to my feet and ran the cold water, ducking my mouth under the spigot to take a long, long drink.

I ran a hand down my clothes on the towel rack. The underwear was mostly dry, but the leggings were drenched. Still, I didn't like being half-naked. I painstakingly put them on and shivered at the chill, wishing I could wear my sweater instead of using it for a sling.

The second I got rescued, I would gladly torch the whole freaking ensemble.

Upstairs, a door slammed. Then, voices.

I opened the bathroom door and peered out. All was as I'd left it.

I climbed onto the bed. Out the window, the tractor was still there, as was the diced ruin that used to be my red Audi. But there was something new.

Something blue was in front of the tractor. With one foot, I kicked the pillow over and stepped on top of it, giving myself another half an inch of height, hoping to increase my vantage point.

The back of a navy car. I could make out the tires, the wide yellow stripes that began above them and—

"Oh my God." The only cars like that were . . .

State Patrol. The State Patrol was here!

Footsteps pounded, descending.

As quickly as I could, I dropped to my knees on the bed, wincing at the shot of pain. I quickly sat down and straightened out my legs, leaning against the head of the bed.

Click!

The door slammed open.

Mrs. Dixon practically snarled, "You need to go in the bathroom."

I glanced over at the open bathroom door. "Why?"

She shook her head as she strode over to me. "You just need to." She grabbed my good arm and pulled me to my feet. I tried to keep up, but I was weak. Since I wasn't going fast enough for her, she half dragged me until I stood in front of the bathroom sink.

I turned to her. "Why do—"

She yanked the door shut in my face. "Stay in there and be quiet, or I will hurt you." Her footsteps receded, and the outside door slammed.

I sat down on the toilet. I could start screaming right then. Would it do any good? The thick concrete walls of the basement would prevent sound from reaching the front yard or wherever the cop was.

But then from inside the house came more voices. One was definitely deep enough to belong to a man.

I didn't care if Mrs. Dixon would hurt me; I had to take a chance. I yanked the door open and ran over to the basement door, pounding with my good hand. "Hey! Hey let me out!" I yelled as loud as I could, and then stopped to see if anyone came.

No one did.

I screamed, and then stopped to catch my breath.

Were those footsteps?

I ran back inside the bathroom and pushed the door shut.

A second later, the bathroom door opened so hard into me that I nearly fell. She shoved me farther back into the bathroom. "I told you to be quiet!"

A man called from outside the door of the room. "Peg? What's going on?"

She shut the door. "Nothing."

As loud as I could, I yelled, "Help! Help me! She's keeping me prisoner!"

More footsteps, heavier footsteps. The door flew open.

I sank to my knees.

An officer in full patrolman regalia, complete with gun in holster. He was tall, around six one maybe, his dark hair buzzed short. His left hand was flat on the door, thick silver band on his ring finger.

His mouth fell open.

"Oh, thank God," I said. "She's keeping me prisoner!" I

pointed at my face. "She did this to me! And her kid hit me with a stick! I want to go home and—"

His eyes left mine as he slowly turned to the woman. "Jesus Christ, Peg. What did you do?"

She stood there, arms crossed, and slowly shook her head. Not exactly the body language of a kidnapper who had been caught by a law enforcement official.

He frowned. "Peg? Something to say?"

She reached over in front of him and pulled the door shut.

I grabbed the knob and tried to pull. "Help! Get me out of here! Arrest her!"

But the door didn't budge. So I put my right ear to the door and listened.

The cop sounded pissed. "What the hell? Who is that? She looks all beat up."

"She was in a car accident. We brought her here to help her out."

"Bull. She doesn't sound like someone who is here voluntarily."

"She's the one I told you about."

What did that mean?

Had Mrs. Dixon—Peg—called him earlier about the accident? But then why didn't he help me?

He said, "You know I can't turn a blind eye."

Was this her husband? He couldn't knowingly let her keep me, could he?

But then Peg said, "You *will* turn a blind eye. You won't say a word."

A chill ran up my spine.

"Peg, you know I have to report—"

"I'll tell her. I will. I'll call your wife and tell her about us."

I sucked in a breath.

The cop *was* married. But not to her. They were having an affair, and he would stay quiet about me or else . . . Peg would tell his wife.

I hit the door. "Please! You can't let her do this! My name is Olivia Flynn! Everyone will be looking for me!"

There were murmurs, followed by quick footsteps clambering up the steps. "Hey! Don't go! Let me out!" I leaned my forehead against the door. "Come back!"

This isn't happening.

But moments later, a car started up, followed by the crunch of tires on gravel.

I sat down on the closed toilet. My face scrunched up as the first sobs began, so violent they made my shoulder hurt more than it already did. If an actual officer of the law wasn't going to save me, who would?

I jumped when the bathroom door swung open. Peg stood there.

I exploded off the toilet. "You can't keep me here! He's probably going to turn you in."

She smiled. "No, he's not."

"He's a cop! He'll do the right thing!" I yelled.

Peg laughed. "Maybe if he thinks with his head, but trust me, sweetie, he doesn't think with his head. No man does."

I glared at her. "How can you be so evil?"

The smile left her face. "I'm not."

"Really?" I couldn't stop the guffaw that chewed its way out. "Oh my God. First you kidnap me and keep me here. And now you're also having an affair with a married man." I rolled my eyes.

Peg hauled off and slapped me, the smack loud in the quiet room.

I staggered back with the force of it, holding my hand to my stinging cheek.

She jabbed her finger at me. "YOU do not get to judge. YOU have no right. YOU have no idea what it's like."

Even after all she'd already done, I was still stunned that she actually hit me. I mumbled, "What?"

"To be me." She was no longer yelling. "To do everything right, to play by every rule, only to have your husband leave you." She shook her head. "And Ritchie?" She held a thumb up toward the ceiling. "He's one of the only good things in my life. His wife is horrible. He never should have married her. But if he ever leaves her, she'll take him for everything he has."

"Especially if he's an adulterer," I said.

Peg lifted and lowered a shoulder.

"So he won't say a word about the fact you're keeping a prisoner in your basement." Reality hit me. The hope I harbored about the cop—Ritchie—doing the right thing was hollow.

101

She set her hands on her hips. "That's right. So if you're sitting down here thinking he's going to come to your rescue, you might as well forget it. He needs to keep his wife happy." She raised her eyebrows. "And I'll keep him happy."

Not really wanting details about how that was going to happen, I shoved past her and walked over to the bed and sat down. I glanced up at the window. "I know what you did to my car."

"Yeah. Couldn't leave it out on the road. It was a hazard to traffic." She smiled. "Such a shame no one will see it. I mean, if that's what you were counting on."

I narrowed my eyes and glared at her.

She stepped toward the door and put her hand on the handle, starting to leave. But then she paused a second and faced me once more. "It's all so . . . hopeless for you." She shrugged. "Kind of makes you want to pull your hair out, doesn't it?" She slipped out, shutting the door.

The padlock clicked before I could even get my breath back.

She knows.

I crawled into the bed and pulled the covers up.

She knows, she knows, she knows.

Peg knew about the trichotillomania. Which meant she had found the journal. There was no other way she could have known.

My gaze went to the window above my head. There was a smear there, a dirty tongue-shaped smear. I shivered, then yanked the covers all the way over my head and cowered.

Who was that boy in the window? Was he going to come back? Was he something else I had to worry about?

Because I had enough goddamn problems already.

A cop had been there, had known I was being held against my will, and he did nothing. The whipped SOB wasn't going to help me. And my car, my poor wrecked car. The one thing I thought would lead help to me was no longer of any use.

And *now* . . . Peg had found my journal. My secret history.

My body began to rock back and forth.

I am screwed. So clearly and utterly screwed.

12

I HUDDLED IN my cave, unable to do anything but stare at the white wall of sheet inches in front of my face. My stinking breaths were loud puffs in my pathetic little fake haven of safety.

The door upstairs slammed, and there were voices. Peg's and Flute Girl's.

Clunk.

A car door?

Clunk.

Another.

An engine started. Gravel crunched and the sound of the motor receded until there was silence. Were they both gone?

Slowly, I lifted the edge of my cocoon and revealed myself with an automatic glance up at the window to make sure the glass was empty. No jack wagon leering in at me. I breathed a sigh.

I went over to the door and put my ear against it. Nothing. Were they gone?

Where?

It was morning. I quickly added up the days in my head. Sunday. Were they at church?

I rolled my eyes at the irony.

My hand gripped the doorknob and turned. Nothing.

I jiggled it and pushed. Nothing.

Despite its crap appearance, the door wouldn't give.

Obviously, I wasn't going anywhere.

"Can one freaking thing go my way? Please?" I leaned back against the door, studying the basement. There had to be something I hadn't noticed. Something I could use to get out. Now would be the time to explore because I could make as much noise as I wanted without alerting anyone.

Over at the table, I pried a lid off one of the plastic containers. I found small bottles of paint and some brushes. Also some stamps, like my mom had for scrapbooking. Not that she ever used them, mind you. But when scrapbooking was hot, she bought all the accoutrements in case the urge struck her.

I dug through, hoping for a forgotten pair of scissors. Maybe an X-Acto knife. I raised my eyebrows. *Yeah. Now that would be a seriously wicked weapon.* One whole side of the container was a stack of paper. One sheet looked like a smeared rainbow of pastels, pink and blue and green.

In seventh-grade art, we'd made paper like that. First we spread out sheets of tissue paper and dripped food coloring on them. The dots immediately drifted outward, diluting in color. We let them dry until the next day and then ironed sheets of waxed paper on top. Our teacher had to help, of course. I suspect that letting a bunch of twelve-year-olds play with a heavy, hot iron without supervision would have been frowned upon. But the end result was a sheet of what resembled pretty, handmade paper.

Did Peg actually let Flute Girl loose with an iron?

I let go of the sheet and let it drift down to the rest of the stack, then replaced that container's top and popped off another. Nothing but books. I picked one up and looked at the cover.

The Quest for the Coven by J. M. Cutler.

My groan was instantaneous.

"Seriously?" Of all the books in the world, this one had to end up in my basement prison?

That particular young adult novel had come out about six months after *The Caul and the Coven*, the first book of my trilogy. There were enough similarities in it to mine that my mom and I had actually considered litigation, until Billy had talked me out of it.

But I mean, come on. Two kids, looking for their lost mother, who was trapped in a gemstone from a necklace? And then they needed to hunt down the rest of the missing gems and put them back in the necklace in order to get their mother back?

Sounded suspiciously like mine, except in *The Caul and the Coven* the mother was trapped in a set of books. I read the Cutler book, of course. I wanted to see what it was about. The writing wasn't all that bad, but what a rip-off.

My book was already on the *New York Times* bestseller list, and Billy thought that it might seem petty of me to pursue a lawsuit and that I would look better in the press if I ignored it. But I chose to write a blog entry about it.

That post resulted in many of my fans going into a bit of a frenzy, crucifying J. M. Cutler as a plagiarist. They went on all the online review sites for readers and wrote horrible reviews of his books. I felt kind of bad about it. But J. M. Cutler never came forward or posted a rebuttal of any kind. Billy said he thought that J. M. Cutler was a pseudonym, probably made up by a book packager looking to cash in on a hot property.

I dropped the book back in the bin and quickly perused some of the other titles. Most were YA. I'd read many of them, since I liked to keep up with the competition. At least I would have something to pass the time if I wanted. I set the lid back on top. Books, art supplies. Other than the starvation, pain, torment, and torture, this incarceration was turning out to be almost like summer camp.

I rolled my eyes. I could read a book, paint a picture, maybe even make some fancy paper if I felt so inclined—

I gasped as something suddenly dawned on me.

I ripped off the top of the container with the paper in it. I quickly dug through the stack, searching. Nothing. Nothing but paper.

"Where is it?" I shoved that tub aside and went to the only other one I hadn't rummaged through. "Please. Be there." Wax paper. A wax paper box had a slicing edge on it that was sharp as hell.

I pulled off the top.

"Yes!"

If there had been clouds in that basement, they would have parted and a heavenly choir would have kicked in, singing "Hallelujah!" at the top of their lungs. Because there, resting on top, was a blue box of Cut-Rite Wax Paper. For the first time in the past couple of days, something had actually gone my way.

I reached into the plastic tub and lifted out the box, quickly flipping up the top to view the cutting edge. I raised my eyebrows at the warning. *Caution: Cutting Edge Is Sharp. Avoid Contact.*

A smile spread across my face.

Another phrase declared: *The Perfect Kitchen Assistant.* "Oh, buddy, if all goes well, you're going to be assisting me in something far more nefarious."

Carefully, I tore the cardboard, pulling off the front of the box with the whole cutting edge. The thing rolled up, wilting in my hand. Too long to be of any use. So I bent the metal back and forth, attempting to break off a length that could be easily concealed.

Finally, the metal strip snapped in two.

I smiled and stuffed the rest of the strip into the wax paper box, then closed it, and placed it back into the container, shoving it under a ball of red yarn. I replaced the top of the tub and straightened it and the others so that they appeared untouched.

The tub of books tempted me. A lot. But if they found me

reading, they'd know I'd been snooping. They might look to see if I'd taken anything else.

That couldn't happen.

Back at the bed, I reached down and slipped the slim strip of metal and cardboard between the mattress and the box spring, pushing only far enough to hide it. I slid my fingers in the gap to check. The strip was right there, easily within reach of my good hand.

Okay. Okay.

Without looking, I reached down and took it out, then put it back. Then I did it all over again. And again and again, until I knew exactly where to reach.

Leaving the cardboard attached had been a smart move because it gave me something to hold on to. Otherwise the strip would have been unwieldy and sharp. I found my best grip was holding it between my thumb and forefinger. Then I practiced slashing at the air.

It wasn't much of a weapon, but it could buy me a moment. A moment was all it took to slip out the door. And if I could get out that door, I knew I could make it out and find help. I knew I could.

I put my weapon away and leaned back against the headboard. My stomach growled.

I slid down and curled up, pulling the covers over me.

I didn't even care anymore that I was hungry. My hunger fed me, fueled my rage. Because I was past being a victim. One way or the other, I was getting the hell out of here.

¤ ¤ ¤

I MUST HAVE DRIFTED OFF. THERE WAS A TAP ON THE WINDOW.

Had they come back without my hearing the car? Was Flute Girl messing with me?

My heart pounded as my gaze drifted upward.

I gasped. The boy was back, the boy from last night. He had short brown hair, dark eyes, and a huge, leering grin. My whole body buzzed. I scrambled off the bed and ran into the bathroom, shutting the door. I pressed my back against it, my heart jumping like crazy.

Oh my God.

For the first time ever, I wanted Peg to come back. Even Flute Girl would have been fine. I didn't want to be alone there with *him*, whoever he was.

A minute later, a door upstairs banged shut, and then the ceiling creaked. I pressed my ear to the bathroom door.

Footsteps on the stairs, heavier than either Peg's or Flute Girl's.

He is coming downstairs.

BANG!

I jumped and gasped.

He'd hit the door. Or kicked it. Then the doorknob sounded like it was being jiggled. He mumbled something, sounded like a swear word I didn't quite catch.

He kept jiggling.

My heart threatened to pound out of my chest.

What if he got in? There was no way to lock the bathroom door.

I *could* make a move for the weapon in my bed. But how much of a weapon would it be against this guy? I'd only seen his face, but he was obviously capable of running whatever machinery was needed to cut up a car. And given how weak I was, my own grandmother could have taken me at that point.

He spoke again. "Where is it?"

What was he looking for?

The door banged again, like he'd kicked it. "I'll find the key, and then I'm coming in there," he shouted.

I swallowed. He was looking for the lanyard with the key. I whispered, "Please, please, let Peg have it with her."

Then all his sounds stopped.

Until he called out, "So what are you doing, Oh-liv-ee-aah?"

He knew my name.

I hated the way he said it. I held my breath, hoping he'd give up and go away when I didn't answer.

He asked again, in a singsongy way. "Oh-liv-ee-aah, what are you do-ing?"

My skin crawled.

He rapped on the door.

Shave and a haircut. Two bits.

I shivered.

"I'm gonna get in there. Just a matter of time, Oh-liv-ee-aah."

I slid down to a crouch, hugging myself with my good arm.

"Little pig, little pig, let me come in."

Not by the hair of my chinny chin chin, you douche bag.

"Let me in." He did the singsongy thing again. "We'll have some fuh-un. . . ."

My chin began to wobble.

A tear slipped down my cheek. I swiped it away. "Stop it," I whispered. "He can't get in." Peg was a planner, I'd give her that. She had made my prison secure.

He growled and smacked the door. "Stupid Peg. She told me I could have some fun."

Under my breath, I said, "Go away."

He kept talking. "I'm actually a nice guy. Really."

I doubted that.

"We could play a game of chess."

Sure we could.

The weird thing was, his voice sounded almost like someone I knew. Maybe an actor on television, or the movies.

I let out a shallow breath.

Then a blast of music, insanely loud, with a male voice screaming words I couldn't even understand. I slapped my hands over my ears, wincing at the pain in my left shoulder. So I could only cover one ear. The singer's voice was raspy and rough, the drumbeat rapid, the bass booming. My heart raced faster.

I stood up and grabbed a hand towel, wrapping it around my head.

The music got louder, beating its way into my body. "Stop it!" I yelled.

Two doors stood between me and the sound, and it still hurt my ears. How could he stand to be so close to it?

There was a faint rapping. How had I even heard it over the deluge? I cracked open the door enough to see him pounding on the window.

As soon as he noticed me, a grin spread across his face. He waved: one quick flat slice of his hand through the air. Then he disappeared.

Gone. He was gone.

I ran to the bed and grabbed a pillow. Back in the bathroom, I slammed the door, dulling the music only slightly. He'd left me with that sound, that sound so violent it vibrated through my body. I closed the toilet lid and dropped the pillow on top of it, then got down on my knees. I bent over, lay my left ear on the pillow, then pressed a towel to my right ear, and cradled that side of my head with my arm.

But the sound still trembled through my skin and kept my heart pounding so that I couldn't even think. Not that I wanted to think.

Because when I did, the only thing that bounced about in my head was this: How many ways would these people come up with to torture me? And what could I have possibly done to deserve it?

13

I WAS SO exhausted that I couldn't do anything but lie there, feeling the noise burrow into my body. My back and legs began to cramp up. But I didn't want to move. Uncovering my ears even for a second was out of the question. My lower back began to scream, and my bad shoulder was killing me. I had to sit up. I had to—

Silence.

I was afraid to believe it. Slowly, I lifted up my arm and pushed aside the towel on that ear.

My ears rang. My head ached. But there was no more music.

Was it a trick? Would he turn it back on as soon as I thought it was over? Toy with me until I was more of a wreck than I already was?

I tensed up, ready to flop back down to protect my ears.

Click!

Was the music a distraction? Had he found another way to get the door open?

I sat up and crawled to the bathroom door. My legs were sore from being bent for so long.

He couldn't get in. I wouldn't let him.

I held my breath, braced myself for his shoving his way through the door. I should have gone out and gotten my weapon. Why the hell didn't I?

"You can come out; I turned that crap off."

Peg.

The breath whooshed out of me.

I was actually glad to hear her voice. Yes, she was my enemy, but I was pretty confident she wasn't capable of . . .

Well, I'd rather tolerate anything she dished out than whatever that boy had in store for me. I realized that for the first time, I thought of Peg as my protector instead of my captor. I knew it was dangerous thinking. But maybe it would keep me alive.

I turned the knob and opened the door.

Peg stood there in a blue-flowered dress that revealed her figure. Her hair was up in a bun. Swear to God, if she hadn't been the reason I was stuck in that basement, she could have been a normal person, back from church. Someone who baked pies for the potluck and watched the babies in the nursery.

She said, "I didn't mean for that to happen."

Was she apologizing?

Because she didn't seem all that remorseful. In fact, she seemed kind of smug.

Not really expecting her to answer me, I asked, "Who is he?"

She shook her head, like it was inconsequential. "My cousin. He lives . . . around here. Helps me out now and then."

Her cousin?

"He dragged my car in."

I wasn't asking.

"And cut it up." She shrugged. "He's good for things like that."

I didn't want to know what he was bad for. Mustering my confidence, I announced, "I don't want him anywhere near me."

Her eyes narrowed. "I don't care what you want."

"Really? You're fine with him torturing me?" Heat rushed up my face, and I raised my voice. "Because there will be a reckoning for this. There will."

Peg shrugged. "He's harmless." She held out a white bag that I hadn't noticed in her hand. "Here."

I didn't move.

She rolled her eyes. "Fine, I'll take it back if you don't want it."

I snatched the bag from her hand. It was heavier than it looked, and I nearly dropped it.

Her eyebrows raised, and a smirk crossed her face. "What, no thank-you?"

"Thank you," I whispered.

She turned and left.

Click.

My legs were still stiff as I limped over to the bed and sat down. Placing the bag on the bed, I stared at it a moment as I rubbed my hand along my leg.

The bag looked like it was from a bakery.

Could I trust her?

Could there be food in the bag?

Absolutely, there could be food in that bag.

But there could just as easily be a dead, bloody squirrel or something equally nasty inside.

I sighed. I'd seen that in movies, too.

My mouth watered and my stomach growled.

Because it would be just like them to do something even meaner than they'd already done.

I set a hand on the folded top of the bag.

"You don't know what's in there."

I licked my lips.

Unable to stop myself, I flipped up the fold on the bag. I opened it, and then shut my eyes. "Okay. On three. One. Two."

Please oh please oh please . . .

"Three." My eyes slowly opened to peek at the contents.

Two glazed doughnuts and a small blue carton of milk, 2 percent.

"Oh my God." I shoved one doughnut in my mouth and bit down, barely chewing the sweet softness before I swallowed, basically inhaling it. Another bite, then another, until it disappeared. "Mmmmmmm." Sugar lingered on my lips, and I licked them, and then sucked the sweetness off my fingers. I wedged the milk carton tightly between my legs and opened it with one trembling hand. I lifted it to my mouth and took several swigs before I could stop myself.

I set it down.

"Slow down." I didn't know when I'd get fed again. *If* I'd

get fed again. Slowly, I closed the top of the bag, folding it along the crease. I set the bag at the end of the bed.

There. I would save the other doughnut.

My gaze went to the milk carton. Warm milk sucked. I tilted my head back and put the carton to my mouth, shaking it until every drop had landed in my mouth. I swallowed and then burped a moment later. My stomach wasn't even close to being full, my hunger nowhere near being squelched.

I stared at the white bag for several minutes. Then I lay down and curled up, pulling the covers up to my shoulders. A nap. A nap would make me feel better. And having something in my stomach was a comfort, even if it was only a little something.

I shut my eyes.

What if they came in while I was sleeping? What if they took the bag away?

My eyes snapped open. I grabbed the bag and tucked it into my chest. The bag crinkled whenever I moved. I liked hearing it, knowing it was there. Knowing I had something that was mine.

Ironic. Because in the outside world, yeah, I owned plenty of things. Most people would have called me materialistic, and rightly so. I had a veritable crap load of things.

Peg had no clue what I could do. When I got out of there, I would do that *Today* show interview. I would fry her and her stupid cousin and Flute Girl. The entire country would be behind me, feel sorry for me, and want to hear my story. And I would tell it.

Oh, would I tell it.

People magazine would want to do an exclusive. A cover story! Or I could do a book about it. A memoir. Billy could get me big bucks for it, I bet.

I just had to get through this and make it out.

I shut my eyes and listened to the creaking floorboards overhead, the muffled voices of Flute Girl and Peg. The tension in my shoulders began to relax.

Now I found their voices reassuring? Only the day before, the same sound had me on edge. But the difference was that I'd recently discovered there were potentially worse things than Peg and Flute Girl. And as long as those two were up there, that boy couldn't get to me.

But I knew the longer I stayed in the basement, the more chances he would have to break in when they weren't home.

How long were they going to keep me there?

I slid my hand out to the edge of the mattress and over, slipping my fingertips into the gap above the box spring.

They brushed the edge of the blade. I left them there for a second, against the sharp metal, pressing. There was no doubt in my mind that if I pressed hard enough, I would draw blood.

Satisfied, I withdrew my hand.

Whatever happened next, at least I was armed.

And I wouldn't just lie there. Not anymore.

14

THE WHITE PASTRY bag crinkled as I cuddled it. Given my level of exhaustion, I should have passed out immediately. But that didn't happen.

I sighed and rolled over on my back, staring up at the ceiling. I set the white bag on my stomach. At least, with the blade concealed beneath me at that very moment, I felt a little more powerful. Maybe I wasn't exactly in control of the situation, but it was only a matter of time. Peg would slip up, and I'd make my move.

And then, once I got out . . .

What? What would I do? Go back to everything the way it was?

Books. Movie deals. Packing for college.

After this, the thing I wanted most was to just get home and stay there. Was that weird?

Maybe I needed to go to the U. of O., make friends.

But I didn't want to be anyplace else new. I didn't want to deal with strangers. I wanted to be home.

I swallowed.

I don't ever want to leave home again.

Was that the truth?

I scratched my head. But I was so excited to go to school. I'd registered for classes; I had my own room in the best dorm on campus. It all sounded perfect.

Sounded perfect.

Did it feel perfect when I thought about it?

Or was I doing it simply because it was expected of me?

Was college something that I wanted, or was it something my parents wanted? What did I actually *want* anyway?

First, to get out of that hellhole of a basement. Second, to make Peg and Flute Girl pay for what they did to me, what they put me through.

I sighed.

Okay. But what then?

Go back home, finish my novel, and pack for college.

"I don't want to go to college."

I slapped a hand over my mouth. Had I said that aloud?

I tested the words one more time, slowly. "I . . . don't . . . want . . . to . . . go . . . to . . . college."

Those words felt good. I raised my eyebrows. "Okay. So that's what you don't want to do. What do you want to do?" I bit my lip for a moment. "I want to go see Rory."

Those words sent a rush of heat up my chest that bubbled over and out into a weird sound that was a cross between a gasp and a sigh. "I do. I want to go see Rory." My parents hadn't wanted me to. I was too young, they thought.

"I'm almost eighteen!" I shook my head. "I've got the money."

I had more than enough to take a trip to Chicago. I could afford to do whatever I wanted. Why hadn't I stomped my foot before this? Told my parents I was going to see him and that was it?

Maybe I needed to be locked in a basement and tortured before I would finally stand up for myself. Because after this, I wasn't doing a damn thing I didn't want to. And I was going to do whatever I pleased, including flying to Chicago to see my boyfriend.

I began to imagine it: getting off the plane, heading to baggage. Rory standing there, holding flowers—maybe yellow roses, my favorite—and his smile spreading as he noticed me. His dimples would burst out, melting my heart. I would take a step into his strong arms and then his lips would press against mine. Our first kiss.

I stopped. The image left my head. Did I really believe that would happen? Did I really believe he loved me?

"He loves me. He told me he loves me." But he'd never met me in person. We'd never talked in person. He'd never smelled me or touched me or seen the way I walk. I'd never smelled or touched or seen the way he walked, either, but it didn't matter. I'd been talking to him once a week for months upon months. That was all I needed.

I sighed.

So then why did I think it wouldn't be enough for him?

Because there was a possibility, a slight one rolling around in my head, that if I weren't a bestselling author, he wouldn't want anything to do with me.

Granted, he'd never wanted anything from me. I'd offered

so many times to buy him a new computer, but he always turned me down. But what if the thing that attracted him to me was that I could write a decent novel? Would we be Skyping if I was simply some girl?

No.

Would I even be on his radar?

No.

Would he still think I was beautiful? Would he still tell me he loved me?

I didn't know the answer to that. I would never know the answer because I *was* a bestselling author and that was how he found me. I needed to be confident, to believe that I was capable of being beautiful to him, that I was worthy of being loved by him.

I nodded.

I *was* capable of being beautiful.

I had to be worthy of being loved.

And when I got home, I would take control of everything. First would be not going to college. Why should I? My career wasn't going to get better with a college degree. Hell, I was doing things that the typical college graduate could only dream about.

And second . . .

Second would be Rory. I'd book a flight, go to Chicago, and get the nicest, most expensive hotel room in the city. Because meeting Rory for the first time? A kiss wouldn't be enough, I didn't think. A kiss wouldn't be nearly enough. All those Sunday nights of—

I sat up, grimacing at the pain the quick movement caused. *Today is Sunday.*

Rory would be waiting for me to Skype!

What would he think? That I was blowing him off? I'd never missed one Sunday night, ever. He had missed one when his grandmother died. And another when he had the flu. I had understood.

I squeezed my eyes shut. Peg couldn't have planned that any better. One more thing for me to lose, thanks to her. "No." I opened my eyes. Even if they'd had to wait twenty-four hours to officially declare me missing, that time had passed. My disappearance would have at least made the news by now. And Rory would know I was missing, that I wasn't bagging our Skype.

He would know. And he would wait for me. Because he loved me. He'd told me so, even after I told him everything about myself. I had to believe him.

And I had to suck it up and use all my energy to get out of there. Because I knew he was waiting for me.

That was the first thing I would do. Go see Rory and find out that our feelings for each other were true.

15

FINALLY, I DOZED off. When I woke up, the light outside wasn't as bright. Evening. Sevenish, I guessed. The bag crinkled as I moved. "Oh crap." In my sleep, I'd rested my arm on it.

I opened the bag and pulled out the doughnut. One half was flattened. I shrugged and took a bite. Ugly or not, the taste was still as light and sugary as before. Despite trying to pace myself, the doughnut was gone four bites later. I licked my lips and sucked my fingers, determined not to waste the remaining morsels of sweetness.

My throat was dry, so I went into the bathroom and took a long drink from the sink. I turned off the water and stood up, wiping my mouth with the back of my hand.

In the mirror, my face looked haggard and beat up. Dark shadows lay under my eyes, and the long scratch on my cheek was still red. But all the little cuts were scabbing over, as if they had come from a session of half-assed shaving.

"Lovely. You look so lovely." I rolled my eyes at myself.

Click!

I quickly stepped over to the bathroom door, shutting it with a hushed click. I set my ear against it.

The bedsprings squeaked slightly.

Someone was sitting on the bed. Within reach of my weapon.

Crap.

"I brought dinner."

Peg.

Taking my time, I emerged from the bathroom.

She perched on the very edge of the bed. Right above my hidden blade.

My heartbeat sped up, and my hands began to sweat.

A greasy, tomatoey smell wafted toward me. In her hands sat a pepperoni pizza on a cardboard circle. Despite my nerves at her being so near my hidden weapon, my mouth involuntarily watered.

Peg set the pizza on the side table near the bed.

Please get up. Please.

But she stayed put, her hands on the edge of the bed. The weight of her body pushed the mattress downward, meaning her fingers were mere inches above the blade from the waxed paper.

I had to get her away from there. But how?

And then it came to me.

I took a quick step toward the door, an unimpressive, half-hearted juke.

My pathetic move had the intended result. Peg shot off the bed, immediately blocking me from the door. She took a wide stance, hands on her hips. "Really?"

"Sorry." I shook my head. "I wasn't doing anything."

She pointed to the bed. "Go sit down."

I lowered my head in exaggerated meekness, breathing a sigh of relief as my butt sank into the edge of the bed where she had been. For the moment, my hidden arsenal was safe.

Peg nodded at the pizza. "We eat pizza on Sundays."

I nodded. "My family does, too."

We didn't, of course. But I was attempting to cooperate. Because I was ready to try out my weapon and get the hell out of there. My right hand was hidden from her, and I stretched out my arm, sliding my fingers into the narrow gap.

My fresh, docile tone must have allayed her tension because her shoulders relaxed. She stepped a few feet toward me.

My heart pounded so hard that I felt it in my ears. Sweat broke out on my upper lip, and I quickly faked a cough so I could wipe it off as I covered my mouth. Then my hand snapped back to my side, fingers slipping in and grabbing the blade as Peg neared.

Patience. Hold on.

I needed to get her talking, distract her. "So how much longer do I have to stay down here?" I maneuvered the blade into my palm, then between my thumb and forefinger. I tightened my grip. I wanted to add, *Because I'm about ready to take my leave, bitch.*

She frowned. "I don't know." She stopped walking toward me.

No! I swallowed the despair climbing up my throat.

I needed her near me, away from the door, so that when I attacked I'd be able to get to the door before she did.

Peg tilted her head. "You haven't shown any regret for what you did."

My mouth fell open, and I almost dropped the blade. I got a firmer hold on it and gathered my wits. Was she kidding me? Were we back to that? "I apologize for whatever it is I did."

She set a hand on her forehead and rubbed a little as she shut her eyes. "No, see, that is what"—her eyes shot open and she jabbed her hand in the air at me—"PISSES ME OFF!"

I jumped at her sudden rage. One of my feet slid forward on the slick carpet, and I nearly slid off the bed.

She took a few steps toward me, arms out to the sides, her face reddening. "Do you think this is easy for me? Having a stranger in my house that I have to feed?" She closed in on the bed, only a foot or so away from me. I could have reached out and touched her.

I sucked in a breath. *Here we go.*

"This isn't easy for me! Do you think I want you here?" she yelled.

I shook my head, trying to appear complacent, attempting to calm her down.

Because I hadn't been prepared for her to be angry. An angry person is unpredictable. I couldn't blow my last chance at getting out.

"I have a daughter to worry about, in case you haven't noticed!" Peg's voice grew louder. She took another step toward me, cutting the distance to about a foot. She was so close that

I could see the outline of her bra underneath her dress and a bit of mascara on the outside of her eye. I smelled her perfume, an overpowering, almost invasive scent.

Peg sighed. "You are not the only problem I have."

I bit my lower lip and tried to keep my hands from trembling.

Should I do it?

Worst-case scenario if I screwed up again? She hurts me, maybe a lot, takes away my weapon, and . . . what else? What more could she do?

Restrain me somehow. Tie me up.

I fought back a shudder as I remembered the gag in my mouth.

Being trapped in the basement was bad enough, but at least I was free to move around. If I had to be down there and be tied up, maybe even gagged again? I would lose it.

I couldn't take that chance.

Slowly I slid my hand beside my thigh and over the edge to stow my weapon.

"This is your entire fault!"

That stunned me. "What?" As I turned to look up at her, I lost hold of the strip. My salvation fell to the floor, landing silently beside my foot. My heart stopped.

Don't look at it, don't look at it.

I quickly stood up and stepped on the metal and cardboard, covering it with my foot. I held out my palm in submission. "I'm sorry for whatever I did, okay?" All I needed to do was stay there until she left. That's all. Keep it covered, and she would never know.

Peg stepped back and set a hand on the post at the end of the bed. "Not good enough." She shook her head. "Not nearly good enough."

She grabbed my wrist and yanked. I stumbled forward, stepping off the one thing that I was trying to keep hidden.

I didn't dare look back. The blade was behind me, completely out in the open. I had to get her away from that side of the bed. So I did the first thing that came to mind. Stupid, maybe, but I was desperate, and it had to be done.

With my good arm, I shoved her as hard as I could.

Peg stumbled back a step. Her hair fell over her eyes, which narrowed at me.

What was I thinking? A little metal strip against this walking, talking, raging grudge bitch?

Peg raised her arm, and I covered my face with my good one. "Don't!" I yelled.

She grabbed my arm, pinching hard with her fingers. I yelped. She pushed down, forcing me to my knees. I dropped, and then fell over on my right side. If she looked past me, she'd see the metal strip lying on the floor. She'd see it and grab it and probably use it on me.

Quickly, I righted myself and scooted a few feet away, toward the other side of the bed. *Please follow me, please follow me.*

She did. With two long strides, she was at my side, away from where she could see my weapon.

I sat up. All I needed was to placate her enough so that she'd leave. Then everything would be okay. I'd try again another time.

Peg kicked me in the stomach.

I doubled over and clutched my midsection, gasping. My mouth opened and closed, opened and closed. But I was unable to take a breath. I fell on my side and waited for my paralyzed solar plexus to relax, let me have oxygen.

Peg leaned down over me. Her face was red, eyes wide and wild. She held up one fist.

My eyes teared up, blurring her face. But not her words.

"Don't mess with me, sweetheart. You got it?"

I lay there, unable to breathe or move or think.

She grabbed a handful of my hair. With it, she pulled me up off the floor about half a foot. I cried out, except that I had no breath at the moment, so there was only a squeak.

"Got it?" she asked.

I nodded as best I could with her clenching my hair. Apparently the movement was a close enough approximation to a nod because she let me go.

I fell back to the floor, still holding my stomach as the first tiny gasp of air began to come through.

"Enjoy your pizza." She left and slammed the door.

Click!

If I had a breath, I would have sighed with relief. But all I could do for the moment was stare up at the ceiling and let the tears leak out of my eyes.

16

AS SOON AS my breath came back, I got up and tightened my sling. Then I knelt beside the bed. With a trembling hand, I picked up the strip of cardboard and metal and slid it back into the gap between mattress and box spring. I lay my palm out flat over the spot and pressed my forehead to it. "Thank you."

Wiping away stray tears, I got up on the bed and grabbed a slice of pizza. I stuffed the end of the triangle into my mouth and bit off a huge piece. I chewed loudly, my mouth open. The crust was thin and brittle; cheese, nearly tasteless; the pepperoni, greasy. Obviously some cheap frozen brand.

Also definitely the best thing I'd ever tasted in my life.

I swallowed and took another bite, chewing with my eyes closed, savoring every minute. That piece was gone quickly. I reached for another. On the third slice, I slowed down a bit and paused halfway through.

"This is your last piece. You need to save the rest."

I didn't want to. Not really. But I needed to listen to myself.

Who knew when she'd feed me again?

Doughnuts and pizza in the same day was encouraging, but maybe they only fed their captives on Sundays. If so, then I was pretty freaking lucky I rolled my car on a Friday.

A door slammed overhead.

I took a bite and listened as I chewed.

A car door shut. Only one. Engine started, tires crunching on gravel.

Peg left. Alone.

I swallowed.

Flute Girl was upstairs. She better stay up there and not bother me. I took the last bite of that piece of pizza. Then I went into the bathroom and took a long drink. When I came out, tires crunched the gravel.

I sat back down on the bed.

Upstairs, a door banged and Flute Girl screeched, but in a happy way. Footsteps ran across the floor. Why was she so happy to see her mom?

I bit my lip. Unless it wasn't her mom.

And then I heard a male voice. Footsteps on the stairs. One set light, quick. Flute Girl.

But the other was heavy, slower. Who was it? And what did he want?

My heartbeat sped up, and my hands began to tremble. Should I stay where I was? In reach of my weapon?

No. It would be useless with two people there.

Should I go into the bathroom and try to barricade the door?

Their voices were outside the basement door. Maybe they

didn't even have the key to the padlock. Maybe Peg took it with her. They couldn't get in without the key.

Click!

I slid off the bed and ran toward the bathroom, thankful for the sling containing my bad arm close to my side so it didn't get jarred too much. I slipped inside the bathroom and shut the door the second the other squeaked open.

"So where is she?"

I sucked in a breath.

That voice. I knew it. Peg's cousin.

"I don't know. Somewhere." Flute Girl.

"That door? Is that a bathroom?" he asked.

Had he never been down there before? How was that possible? If he did stuff for her, stuff he was *good* for, wouldn't he have been in the basement?

What would be the reason for him *not* being in the basement?

Maybe he only helped her do outdoor stuff.

Or else maybe she really did use the room to hold people hostage. Well, other people besides me.

The lock was on the outside. Maybe she just wanted to keep Flute Girl out.

Or maybe she didn't trust him in her house. That's why he hadn't been down there.

Bam!

I jumped as something hit the door.

"We know you're in there," he said.

Bam!

"Might as well come out."

I held my breath.

Then the knob turned, and the door started to open. I shoved back against it, but my feet slid across the floor. I lost my balance and slipped, landing on my butt.

The boy walked in and stood over me. He wore jeans and a black T-shirt with some red Chinese symbols on it. His dark eyes slipped down my body, lingering.

My face burned.

His eyes slid back up to mine. He raised his eyebrows and held out a hand.

I didn't take it.

"Suit yourself." He crossed his arms, shut the door, and leaned back against it.

I slid backward as far as possible, until my back bumped against the wall and my escape reluctantly came to a halt. My voice was breathy as I asked, "What do you want?"

"What do I want?" He laughed. "That's a fine way to treat a guy. What, no introductions? Because that's how this is supposed to work." He set a hand on his chest. With that stupid smirk on his face and a falsetto voice he said, "Why, hello there. My name is Wesley. I'm pleased to make your acquaintance, Olivia."

My name on his lips—in that weird voice—sent a shiver down my neck.

Wesley slid to a squat against the door, his faded jeans

tightening around his solid thighs. His biceps grew more defined as he bent his arms and rested them on his legs. He looked wiry and strong. My only hope was that he was also stupid.

"You should be nicer to me." He shrugged. "I mean, after all, we're already intimately acquainted." His gaze slid to my crotch.

I shivered and blurted out, "Peg will be back soon. She won't like that you're down here with me." I hoped that might make him think.

He tilted his head. "Hmmm . . ." Wesley raised a finger. "I need to correct you there. No, she actually won't be back for a while. Because this is Sunday, and that's the night she has her little rendezvous"—he pronounced it wrong, *ron-dezz-vooz*—"with Deputy Dawg."

Ritchie. Peg was hooking up with Ritchie. I bit my lip.

Wesley raised his eyebrows. "So, no. Sorry to disappoint you. She usually doesn't get home until after ten." He smiled. "That gives us a few hours, at least."

Sweat broke out on my upper lip. I didn't want him to see my hands tremble, so I held my bad arm, giving at least one of my hands something to do.

Where the hell was Flute Girl? She was so nosy. Why wasn't she in here, being a pain in the ass? Maybe I should keep him talking. He seemed like someone who liked to listen to himself.

"How old are you?" I asked.

"Sixteen last month."

Sixteen? *Sixteen?* How the hell did that much slime ooze out of a sixteen-year-old?

Bang! Bang! Bang! "Let me in!"

Flute Girl. Thank God.

Wesley sighed and stood up, then opened the door a bit. Flute Girl stuck her head in. She was chewing something. She reached up and took a bite of the pizza in her hand. *My* pizza that I was saving for later.

"That's mine." I couldn't help it, the words just shot out.

Flute Girl shoved her way in and leaned against Wesley. She batted her eyes at him, and then turned to me. "Why are you in here?"

"I think she was trying to hide from us." Wesley gazed at me. "Isn't that right, Oh-liv-ee-aah?" He drew my name out long and slow, sending a fresh batch of shivers up my spine. "Are you trying to hide from us?"

"Maybe she thinks we'll beat her up." Flute Girl laughed, her mouth full of my pizza.

Disgusted, I looked down at the discolored tile at the base of the toilet. How could I get them to go away? Ask, maybe? "Please leave me alone."

"Alone?" Wesley mimicked me. "Alone? Why do you want to be alone? You've been alone down here this whole time."

Flute Girl piped up. "We came in a couple times."

"Oh well. Then Oh-liv-ee-uh must be good and lonely, huh? Are you lonely?" He walked over to me and nudged my foot with his bare toes. The feel of his skin on mine made goose bumps rise on my flesh. I bent my knees, getting my feet out of his reach. "Go away."

He stepped closer and set his foot on top of one of mine. "I'm just being friendly. You should be friendly back."

Tears welled up in my eyes.

I was helpless. I wanted him to leave. I wanted them both to leave.

"Don't." I slapped at his foot with my right hand, and he jumped back.

Then he laughed. "Touchy little thing, aren't ya?"

Flute Girl laughed. "Yeah. She's touchy."

God, she was a freak. And obviously in some weird kind of cousin love with Wesley.

She shoved the last of the pizza in her mouth and wiped her hands together. With her mouth full, she said, "My show is almost on."

She started to go, then grabbed Wesley's hand and started to pull him. "Come on. You have to watch it with me."

He shrugged at me. "You heard the little lady. She needs me to watch her show. Your loss." He followed Flute Girl out the bathroom door, and then popped his head back in. "So you'll have to wait. But I promise, as soon as she goes to bed, I'll be back." He disappeared.

The basement door shut.

Click!

I got up on my knees. I almost didn't reach the toilet in time to puke up all the pizza I'd eaten.

17

I CLEANED MYSELF up and took a long drink of water. Huddling up in the bathroom and waiting like a frightened little rabbit for Wesley to come back didn't appeal to me, so I went and sat on the bed. My fingers itched to reach down and grab the weapon, have it at the ready.

I resisted the urge.

What if he came in with Flute Girl? He could easily overpower me while she made sure I didn't escape. No, part of the power of my weapon—a huge percentage, in fact—relied on the element of surprise. The shock of the slash, rather than the blow itself, would hopefully buy me a moment to get out the door. And it didn't work if Flute Girl was in the picture.

But I was torn. As long as Flute Girl was in the basement, nothing would happen. Wesley wouldn't hurt me with her there.

Would he?

Who was I kidding?

I was weak, he was strong. I was injured, he was whole. Wesley could do anything he wanted to me. And because of that, I hoped Flute Girl would stick close, not let me be alone with him.

I bit my lower lip.

Except . . .

Getting him alone would give me the best chance of making my escape.

My best chance and my worst nightmare were the same thing: me being alone with him. I leaned against the headboard and bent my knees. I was just so tired and sore. I didn't know how much fight I had left in me. I wanted it to be over. I wanted to be out of here. I wanted to be home.

What would I be doing right then if I were at home?

Getting ready to Skype with Rory.

My eyes filled with tears. Would I ever even get to meet him? I was so stupid to go for so long without meeting. And why in the hell hadn't I sent him a new computer, one with a working webcam so that I could see him when we talked? See the expression on his face when he told me I was beautiful? When he told me that he loved me?

Stupid. I'd been so stupid to accept everything. I'd been so stupid to mistake kowtowing for contentedness. I did whatever everyone else told me to do and accepted it as what I wanted, too.

Why did I never stand up for myself?

If I escaped, *when* I escaped, things would be different. They would. I'd already decided that I wasn't going to college and was going to visit Rory.

That was the tip of the iceberg.

Maybe I would live at home. Maybe not. Maybe I'd move out, maybe build a house. Maybe close to my parents, maybe not.

Whatever I did, wherever I chose to live, would be *my* choice.

If I got myself out of this situation, things would change.

Click!

Every ounce of determination fled my body. I curled my knees tighter, wrapped my good arm around them, and prayed Wesley would leave me alone.

The door opened.

Wesley walked in and closed the door behind him. He set the padlock and OSU lanyard with the key still attached on the bookshelf next to the door. He noticed me staring at the items and said, "I don't trust that little crazy to not lock me in."

Well, if we agreed on nothing else, we certainly seemed to bear the same opinion of Flute Girl.

He crossed his arms and leaned back against the door. "So. What should we do to pass the time?"

I didn't answer. But as much as every fiber of my being wanted to, I didn't look away from him, either. I needed him alone in that room with me. But I was scared to death.

I cleared my throat and said, with more confidence than I felt, "You know you can get in a lot of trouble helping Peg keep me down here."

He shrugged. "Yeah. I don't plan on getting caught, though."

A huff escaped my lips. "Wow, really? And how do you plan on avoiding that?"

"I don't know." His eyes narrowed. "That's not really what you should be worried about."

I gulped, and then raised my chin to appear much bolder than I felt. "And what should I be worried about?"

Wesley laughed. "You are so different down here than—" He stopped.

I frowned. "Different from what?"

He shook his head. "Never mind." He took a few steps toward me.

I stiffened. The weapon should have already been out. I should have had it in my hand because if I grabbed for it now, he'd see me.

Wesley glanced at his watch. "Well, look at that. Nine thirty on a Sunday night." He tilted his head and set a finger on his chin. "What does one do at nine thirty on a Sunday night?"

I knew what I did every Sunday at that time. I Skyped with Rory. Right then, he was sitting in Chicago at his computer, waiting for me to call.

Wesley kept coming and sat down on the end of the bed. "It would be a good time to Skype, don'tcha think?"

I froze. Why would he say that? He couldn't have any idea about me and Rory.

Unless he'd read the journal.

"I bet Rory is soooo bummed he can't talk with you tonight, huh?" He laughed. "Good night, my beautiful girl."

I gulped. That was Rory's line. He always said it when he signed off. "Shut up!" I yelled. "It's none of your business."

Wesley licked his lips. "Let's meet up in Chicago and have our first kiss."

"That's private." My heart pounded. Bad enough that Peg had read my journal, but she let Wesley read it as well? How invasive. Humiliating.

Tears started to form in my eyes. *Stop it, you can't cry in front of him.* But the thought of him reading my journal, where I wrote about everything, including what Rory and I told each other . . . it was too much to bear. I wanted to grab my little blade and cut his head off. "It's between me and him. It's none of your business."

Wesley laughed then. He laughed so hard that his eyes glistened with tears. He leaned over and held his stomach for a moment. His mirth faded to a chuckle. "You know. Did you ever consider he might be fake? Some guy just yanking your chain."

"Rory is real!" I said. "He came to my book signing!"

Wesley chuckled again, some leftover laughter, and widened his eyes. "Oh, okay. My bad. So you've actually met the dude. I take it all back." And then he laughed again.

I didn't say anything. I didn't remember what I'd written in the journal that far back—whether or not I'd mentioned that Rory told me he was at my signing but that I hadn't actually met him in person.

Wesley must have accepted my silence for what it was: confirmation that I hadn't met him. "Oh, so you never met the dude. So he could be someone out there on the interwebz, some chimo perv just whacking off to your scintillating conversation."

I couldn't stop the tears. "He's real. I know he's real." I sniffled.

"Oh, okay," said Wesley, with mock concern. "I wouldn't want you to go to Chicago for your first kiss and not have it happen."

"Shut up." I wiped my face with my right hand. I wanted him to leave. I didn't even want to try and attack him anymore. Or try to escape. I was tired. So tired.

Wesley pointed a finger at me. "I can help you with that." The corners of his mouth turned up, and his eyes glimmered. "That first kiss. I mean, I don't want you to go all the way to Chicago only to discover Rory isn't real. What a disappointment for you."

I shook my head. "He *is* real. I *am* going."

He slid up the bed, cutting the distance between us in two.

"I need you to leave." My voice quavered, and I knew he heard it.

"Are you nervous?" he asked. "About that first kiss?"

"Shut up," I said. "Just go."

Wesley slid once more, coming to a rest right beside me. His firm backside pressed against my leg. He smelled of wood smoke and gasoline.

I tried to slide away.

He leaned in and over my left side, blocking me from going that way. His face was inches away from mine.

I couldn't help but notice that my right side—my right hand, my right arm, everything—was unencumbered. And inches below me lay a sharp-edged piece of metal.

In order to get it while he wasn't paying attention, he would have to be focused on something else. I leaned to my right, making him think I was trying to avoid him.

"Where you going?" he asked. "I'm doing this for you, you know."

My right arm was bent, my hand flat on the mattress.

"Fine," I said.

His eyes widened a little. "What?"

"Fine." I shrugged my right shoulder slightly. "Kiss me. I don't care." Inside, I was cringing. And when he leaned forward and pressed his lips against mine, I wanted to scream.

His lips were warm and chapped. Disgusting. But I forced myself not to move. He must have thought I wanted more. I needed him to be distracted. And sticking his gross tongue in my mouth would be just the ticket.

I tried not to gag as his hot, slimy tongue groped around in my mouth. My right hand slid out, toward the edge of the bed.

Wesley's tongue kept probing. His hand slid up and rested on top of my left breast.

My fingers crept toward the gap between the mattress and box spring.

His fingers spread out and began to squeeze as his tongue continued to assault my mouth. My skin crawled.

Focus, Livvy, focus.

My fingers reached the gap and stopped. I stretched out my arm as far as I could go.

Nothing.

My reach ended what had to be centimeters from the thing that would get me out of all of this. I needed another inch. And there was only one way to get it.

I slid my bottom down, lowering my body and thus, my arm.

Wesley finally took his mouth off mine. "Oh yeah." He slid down and lay on his right side facing me. With his left hand, he tilted my head toward him and put his mouth back on mine. His hand settled on my right breast.

I reached down with my hand and slid my fingers into the gap. I grasped the strip of metal and cardboard and pulled it out. Careful not to move quickly enough to draw attention to what I was doing, I slowly firmed up my grip.

His fingers yanked down the top of my camisole and exposed my breasts.

I bit his tongue. Hard.

Wesley snapped his head back. "Ow! What the hell?" He clapped his hand over his mouth.

"Aaaaahhhhhhh!" I slashed hard at his face with the blade, drawing a scarlet line down his left cheek.

"Oh, you bitch!" He held his cheek with his other hand.

With speed fueled by pure adrenaline, I slid off the bed and ran to the door, shutting out the screaming pain in my shoulder. My blade was secure in my hand, so I reached for the padlock with only my thumb and forefinger, but got the lanyard instead. When I lifted it up, the weight of the padlock caused the key to slip. The heavy padlock dropped with a clunk onto the floor. I glanced back at the bed.

Still stunned, Wesley held his cheek as he sat up, feet swinging for the floor.

Don't look back!

I stooped over, snatched the padlock from the floor, and flung open the door. I leaped through the doorway onto a cement floor. Stark wooden stairs led upward. I pulled the door shut. As it closed, I caught a glance of Wesley nearing it, his face red, and his eyes narrowed and dark.

I flicked the latch on the door into the silver hasp on the wall just as Wesley slammed into the door.

I screamed and dropped the padlock and lanyard, then shoved my injured left shoulder against the door and grimaced at the pain. I leaned down, grabbed the padlock off the floor, and slid the shackle into the hasp. My hand was shaking so badly I couldn't click the padlock shut.

"Let me out!" The door banged again. The padlock was thick, but that silver hasp seemed to give a little each time Wesley slammed into it.

Come on, come on. I tried again to close the padlock. My chest was heaving. My fingers shook on the metal. "Come on, you son of—"

Click!

A louder, much more satisfying sound from my vantage point on this side of the door, that was for sure. I glanced down and pulled my camisole back up. My hand was still trembling.

Wesley yelled, "I wish I could see your face when you find out the truth about Rory!"

"You want the truth?!" I yelled. "You're going to jail for what you did to me! For helping Peg!"

Wesley laughed, a chilling sound. "Sure. I'll be in jail while you go visit your *boyfriend*. Let me know how that goes."

Bang! He slammed into the door.

I stood there and panted as I waited for the pain in my left shoulder to subside. I reached down for the lanyard and threw it into the dark recesses of the basement. The key landed with a faint *ping* on the cement floor. I lifted my eyes to the top of the stairs.

A door sat ajar.

I'd gotten out of the basement room. Step one complete. Now on to the next one, where I had no idea what lay in store for me. I glanced around.

Where did it—

My blade lay on the floor by the door. I retrieved it. *You didn't let me down.*

Then I straightened my camisole, tightened my sling, and began to climb the stairs.

18

THE FIRST STAIR was rough under my bare foot. The wood looked unstained and felt unsanded. I lifted my other foot to the next stair, then let the other join it as I slid my right hand up the railing.

Bang!

I jumped.

The basement door again. Wesley muttered something.

I set a hand over my pounding heart. *Chill. He's locked in. He can't get out.* But that door wouldn't last forever.

I moved up another stair, one foot after the other, being as silent as possible. I prayed they wouldn't creak very much. As I climbed higher and higher, none did. I reached the top of the stairs and set my hand on the knob. I held my breath, pressed my ear to the wood, and listened.

A clock ticked, almost echoing. Grandfather clock maybe? Although I didn't recall hearing a chime the whole time I'd been there. I listened for the hum of a refrigerator, which would indicate the door opened into the kitchen. But there wasn't anything like that. I leaned closer to the door, my nose nearly sticking out the gap. A slightly charred scent lingered over the smell of pizza. Maybe Peg had burned something recently.

Bang!

Wesley again.

I needed to get the hell out of there before he got loose.

I pushed the door open. *Creeeeaaaaak.*

I froze.

I waited a moment to see if anything happened. Nothing did. I stepped out the doorway, leaving the door open. I couldn't help but notice a rusty dead bolt, again on the outside of the door.

Was it a hobby of hers to lock people in the basement or what? Or were the locks on the outside simply outdated child safety precautions, pointless now that Flute Girl was bigger?

That almost made sense.

I focused my attention on my surroundings. The door had opened into a living room, lit by a single lamp with a dusty white shade. A blue microfiber couch and matching chair and ottoman all faced a large television. Two doorways sat at either end of the room, but both were so dark it was impossible to tell where either led.

Bookshelves lined the far wall. As my gaze ran over them, I saw a patch of red in the dim light. I stepped closer. "Oh my God."

I ran over and grabbed my purse off the shelf, clutching it

to my chest. I quickly set it on the back of the couch and dug for my phone. It wasn't there. I sighed and perused the other shelves, wondering if my phone was possibly somewhere nearby. There was a familiar book spine. *The Caul and the Coven* by Livvy Flynn.

You've got to be kidding me. I could find out right then and there if Peg had ever come to one of my signings. If I'd been right, if I'd somehow inadvertently done something to piss her off. I pulled the book off the shelf and opened it to the page I always signed.

My mouth dropped open.

I hadn't written in it, but someone else had, in black Sharpie no less.

LIAR.

I turned the page. Same words, scrawled on that page and the next and the next. Who would do that to a book?

Flute Girl?

I stopped turning separate pages and flipped through the whole thing at once. *LIAR* was written on every freaking page.

I shut the book. It was evidence. Evidence that Peg and Flute Girl had it in for me. I bet one of those CSI people could figure out if the book had been defaced before they locked me in the basement. That was premeditation.

I smiled. I would put her away, and that book would come in handy during the process. Something else red caught my eye. A folder. I pulled it out.

No way.

I had the same one, somewhere at home, with the words:

Los Angeles Novelist
BOOT CAMP

I opened it. First thing I saw was the eight-by-ten photograph, which had been included in the exorbitant fee. My gaze fell on the girl in the middle of the front row with the thick headband and earnest expression.

Me.

Holy crap. We'd been there together?

If Peg remembered me from her critique group, why didn't I remember her?

I held the photo closer and scanned the faces, none of which looked anything like Peg. Then I peered more closely at a mousy-haired woman with glasses. Bleach the hair, change to contact lenses . . .

Peg.

I breathed out.

But what had I done? Why was she so mad at me? Was it simply because I had ended up published and successful and she hadn't?

Was all of this due to jealousy?

Bang!

Fainter from up here, but Wesley was still at it, trying to get out. I needed to go. But I needed to find some shoes first. Maybe mine were there somewhere.

I shoved the folder back on the shelf, stuck the book and my weapon in my purse, and turned around.

I gasped.

Flute Girl blocked the doorway to the left. She concealed something in her right hand, while she firmly clasped that stupid flute in the left. Her eyes were wide, her jaw slackened. Most likely a mirror image of my expression. Obviously, she was just as shocked to see me as I was to see her.

Her eyes narrowed. "I'm telling my mom!"

"Oh, go right ahead, you little freak." I nearly spat out the words as I headed for the other doorway, hoping it led to the outside. But she was on me in a second. She grabbed my left arm and twisted.

I cried out and dropped my purse, which landed with a thunk on the floor. Then I reached for the only thing that would give me a chance. Her flute. I chose well because she immediately let go of my bad arm and grabbed her flute, trying to wrest it away.

But my face was hot, my heart pounded, and I was pissed. I lifted a foot, planted it firmly on her stomach, and shoved. She fell backward, minus the flute, which was clenched firmly in my hand.

I raised my arm over my head and gazed down at her.

On her back, Flute Girl glared, eyes on her flute. She reached out for it with her left hand. "Give it!"

I snarled, "Don't ever mess with me again." And, as hard as I could, I slammed that flute against the wooden edge of the doorway, bending it practically in two.

She screeched a feral shrill that made me stumble back several steps to put some distance between her and myself. I threw the damaged flute toward the basement door. It hit the wood floor with a clatter and slid to the opening of the door. Flute Girl scrambled after it on all fours.

I followed at a run.

She was so intent on grabbing the flute that she didn't notice me come up behind her. I grabbed her and shoved her through the doorway. She caught herself before she tumbled down the stairs. Just as I was closing her in, she reached up, and I finally saw what was in her right hand.

A Hello Kitty cell phone.

I banged the door shut and slammed the dead bolt home, hoping that the rusty thing would hold.

A second later, Flute Girl yelled, "Mama! She got out! She got out!"

I took a deep breath. Time to go.

19

FLUTE GIRL WAS still yelling, on a cell phone I'd been too hurried and clueless to notice. I wanted to yank the door open and rip it out of her hand, but knew that was stupid. I had a window of escape that was, statistically, already cranking shut.

I glanced at the doorways on either end of the room. Flute Girl had probably been in bed, so that one led to the bedrooms, best guess. I headed for the other. The hallway was dark, lit only by the thin stream of light from the living room lamp. I felt for a switch, but didn't find one. I made my way down the hallway, my hand on the wall.

The adrenaline running through my body masked the pain in my shoulder. I came to a door and flung it open. Cooler air hit me, and the feeling of a larger space. It reeked of motor oil.

I felt the wall, found a switch, and flipped it.

A single-stall garage with dark stains on the cement floor. I stepped down the one stair and looked on the wall for an opener. A white box was there, and I punched the button. Nothing.

"Come on." I punched it again. Could those things be locked?

As fast as I could manage, I traversed the hallway back to the living room. As I passed the basement door, there were voices.

Wesley and Flute Girl. Had she let him out?

Bang!

I jumped.

Flute Girl couldn't find the key! Thank God I'd thought to throw it. Still, as soon as she found it, I'd have more trouble on my hands. That dead bolt probably wouldn't hold long if Wesley got at it. Quickly, I took the other hallway, feeling the wall as I went. My hand hit a switch, and light flooded the kitchen. Tiled floor, white kitchen cupboards, a red bistro set with a tall table and two chairs, a vase of white peonies neatly dressing the top of it. Just past that was a door with a window facing outside.

"Thank God!"

I'd have to leave barefoot, but at least I'd escape.

I ran to the door and turned the knob. Nothing. There was a push-button lock in the knob, so I turned it again. It was already popped out, unlocked. Up on the side of the door was a dead bolt. I slammed it open and grabbed the knob again, yanking.

Nothing.

Come on!

There was another mechanism farther up. Then I realized it was locked from the outside. I slammed my fist against the window, causing it to rattle. *Are you kidding me?*

Lights came down the driveway. I ducked. At least I had my weapon and could—

No.

During the scuffle with Flute Girl, I'd dropped my purse in the other room, along with my wax paper cutting edge.

But I didn't dare face Peg unarmed. I wouldn't stand a chance.

A wooden block of knives sat on the cupboard. I squatted and made my way over there. I stood up and yanked out a knife with a quiet *ting*.

The black handle was thick in my hand, the blade odd-shaped and skinny on one end. I swallowed. All that mattered was that it was sharp.

I ran back to the living room.

Downstairs Wesley yelled, "Just look for it, stupid!"

The largest piece of furniture in the room was the couch. I crouched behind it, sliding into the space sideways as far as I could go. My face was nearly flush with the upholstery, which smelled dusty, while my back rested against the wall. Luckily, the lamp was on the other side of the room, leaving me in some serious shadows. Despite the discomfort, my hiding place was sound.

The kitchen door unlocked and opened.

I held my breath.

Rapid footsteps crossed the kitchen floor, then stopped. Something clicked. Did she set something on the counter? Footsteps again, slower this time.

Peg would pass the basement door on her way to me. If

Flute Girl had released Wesley by then, Peg would let them out.

And God knows I wouldn't stand a chance against the three of them.

My best chance—my only chance—was to confront Peg before she got to that door. Before she let them out. I bit my lip and started to slide out.

Wait wait wait.

What if she went down there first?

I could lock her in. I hadn't heard the kitchen door shut, which meant it was open. *Unlocked.* There was no jingling of car keys. They were probably still in her car.

I just had to get out the kitchen door and into her car. Then I could get out of there.

Footsteps entered the living room and paused.

I didn't dare look. She had to be by the basement door. Wesley yelled something and Flute Girl screeched back.

"Where are you guys?" Peg yelled. The dead bolt clunked.

Please please please. Go down there.

The door creaked open.

I shut my eyes and held my breath, listening for her steps on the stairs. *Take a step, take a step.*

I was poised, ready to spring for that door as soon as she started down those stairs. Should I give her five stairs? I nodded. I waited to begin counting her steps.

Come on, go down. Take a step.

But there was no movement at all.

Leaning sideways, inching over, I aligned my right eye at

the very edge of the couch. I went one inch more and peered out.

Peg stood at the door to the basement. She must have changed for her tryst with Officer Ritchie, because her hair was down and curly, and she wore a black tank top and cropped jeans and—

My shoes. My $300 leather ballet flats.

My mouth fell open. *The freaking nerve.*

Peg's forehead wrinkled as she stared at something on the floor. I followed her gaze.

Something red.

My purse.

Peg shot a glance at the shelf where I'd discovered it. She walked over and stuck her hand in the space where my book had been and straightened the red folder beside it. Peg asked, "Where are you, Olivia?"

My chest knotted up.

I slid my head back, so that I was completely behind the couch, my forehead pressing against the back. I tried not to breathe in the dust.

She continued, "I know you're still here because the garage door is broken and you can't get out the kitchen door without a key."

I took a deep breath and tightened my grip on the knife. Maybe Peg would decide that there was strength in numbers and head down the stairs to get Wesley. But if she didn't . . .

The element of surprise could be just as much a weapon as the knife. Combined, I had a chance. I just had to knock her down and get past her. Could I do it? I'd blown it the last time.

I had to get this one right.

I raised the knife.

Don't screw up again. You can't.

No.

I wouldn't.

I took a deep breath and rushed straight toward Peg, screaming as loud as I could.

Completely caught off guard, her eyes widened at the knife, and her mouth fell open. Her hands went up in front just as I charged into her. She stumbled backward and fell over the ottoman, landing on her back.

My legs hit the ottoman, and I tried to stop. But my momentum was too much and carried me forward and over.

I landed on top of her, our faces inches apart.

Peg immediately grabbed my left shoulder and twisted. I cried out and slashed at Peg's face. She dodged and grabbed for my wrist. I had no way to get a better position and still hold on to the knife, so I slashed out again, as hard as I could, aiming for her shoulder.

At the last second, she moved, causing the full brunt of my swing, which included all my anger and frustration of the past three days, to hit her neck instead.

The blade sank in, the softness yielding easily. I gasped and yanked it out, expecting blood to gush. "Oh my God!" The words were out of my mouth before I even registered what I'd just done.

Peg's eyes widened. She clutched at her neck.

But . . .

. . . the blood was only a trickle, not the river I'd expected.

The knife fell out of my hands and landed with a thump on the floor as I rolled off her and backed away on my butt. "I didn't mean to!"

Peg slowly sat up, her face draining of color. She wasn't mortally injured, obviously, but she wasn't 100 percent.

With the help of the chair nearest me, I got to my feet. "I'm leaving now."

She struggled to get up, just as someone touched my back.

I screamed and lashed out with my good arm.

Officer Ritchie quickly grabbed me. "You're fine."

"No! Let me go! I want to go!"

He didn't release his grip on my arm, but he didn't tighten it, either, or make a move to subdue me further. "Miss Flynn, you're fine. I came to make sure she let you go."

I stopped struggling.

Was he for real?

Peg said exactly the thing I was thinking. "What?"

He glanced down at Peg. "You have to let her go. *I'm* letting her go."

Peg braced a hand on the ottoman and got to her feet, her other hand still pressed to her wound. Rivulets of blood ran down her neck. "You can't."

"I can." Ritchie seemed to stand taller then.

Peg glared at him. "I'll tell your wife everything."

He shook his head. "I'll have to deal with that. But this is wrong. I should have let her go as soon as I found out." He shot a glance at me. "I'm sorry I didn't."

Peg locked eyes with Ritchie as she backed up to the wall, then she slowly slid down it until she hit the floor. She shook her head a couple of times, and then shut her eyes. "Fine." She sat there, bleeding, looking defeated for the first time in my presence.

A screech filled the silence, sending chills up my spine.

Flute Girl flew into the room, launching herself at me. She caught me in the stomach and knocked me over, her red, manic face right in mine as she jumped onto my chest.

I cried out in pain. Before I could try to fight her off, she was lifted up, away from me, in Ritchie's strong grip. She kicked and screamed and thrashed, until he flipped her upside down. "Calm down!"

I sat up. My heart was racing again.

But Ritchie was big and strong, and she was a scrawny kid. *It's okay. He has her. This is over.*

I leaned back against the nearest chair, giving myself a moment to breathe before I got to my feet.

"Mama!" Flute Girl refused to quit screaming as she struggled to get out of Ritchie's grip. Her knees were inches from his chin, while her braids nearly brushed the floor. She stopped for a moment and glared over at me. "You killed my mama!"

"No, I didn't!" I pointed at Peg, who had somehow smeared the blood so it looked like she wore a scarlet turtleneck. Still, she was obviously *not* dead. "Look. She's fine. She's right over—"

Flute Girl slammed a fist into Ritchie's groin.

His knees crumpled, and he dropped Flute Girl as he hit the floor. She leaned over him a moment, then scuttled about four feet away, cradling something.

Flute Girl got to one knee and whirled toward me, her eyes, hate filled and flashing, locked with mine.

But I slowly lowered my gaze to the black barrel of the revolver she pointed straight at my face.

A flash of fear ran up my body, paralyzing me.

Ritchie's hand slapped his empty holster. "Hand it over!"

Flute Girl struggled to hold the weapon with both hands. If it weren't for the obvious weight, plus Ritchie's empty holster, I could have talked myself into believing it was only a toy.

I stared at the barrel, then beyond, to her eyes.

I gulped.

All of this and I was going to die anyway?

"I'm serious! Hand it over!" Ritchie's face twisted in pain as he reached out a hand toward her.

"No! I hate her." Flute Girl scrunched up her eyes at me and tightened her grip on the gun.

Peg stood. "Sweetie, give Ritchie the gun."

"No!" Flute Girl got to her feet and took a step back.

I whispered, "She can't fire it, can she?"

Ritchie didn't answer.

Maybe his silence was an answer.

Not good enough for me. "It's got a safety, right?"

Ritchie didn't look my way. "Internal safeties, to prevent an accidental discharge."

"What does that mean?"

His voice was low. "Only an intentional pull of the trigger will fire the gun."

"Well, I think she's got intention!"

Ritchie shook his head slightly and got to his knees, both palms held out toward Flute Girl. "You need to give me the weapon now." He inched forward.

Flute Girl's eyes darted between me and Ritchie. She turned the gun toward him. "Stay back!"

He halted.

Once again, the gun was leveled at my head.

And, apparently, there was no safety to stop her from pulling that trigger. "Please don't . . ." I held the trembling palm of my good hand toward her, a useless shield, but there was nothing else to do.

Please don't kill me.

Ritchie said, "That's not a toy, and you need to give it back to me."

"I know it's not a toy!" Flute Girl waved the gun a bit, and then lowered it for a moment, her arms obviously fatigued from holding it aloft so long. "She hurt Mama and Freddy!"

What? Who the hell is Freddy?

Ritchie asked, "Who is Freddy?"

"My flute!" she screamed.

And then I was staring at the barrel again.

Peg stepped past Ritchie and stopped beside me. "Sweetie." Her voice was shaky. She held out the hand that wasn't on her neck. "Please put the gun down. I'm fine."

"No!" Flute Girl didn't stop glaring at me. "I hate her. I always have."

Always? How did roughly forty-eight hours count as always?

"I want her to go away."

Behind Peg, partially hidden from Flute Girl, Ritchie slowly got his feet under him, a cat ready to pounce.

I needed to keep her attention away from him. "I am!" I said. "I'm leaving, right now."

"It doesn't mean anything!" she yelled. "I want you to go away FOREVER!" Her finger started to squeeze the trigger.

Ohmygodsheisreallygoingtokillme

I screamed.

Ritchie lunged at her.

She saw him coming and whirled, then pulled the trigger.

BANG!

I kept screaming as he landed on top of her and grabbed the gun, holding it high above her as he pinned her with his body.

I breathed out.

It was over.

Flute Girl had missed him.

Flute Girl had missed *me*.

Everything is fine. It is all over.

And then I turned to my right.

Peg lay on her back, legs sprawled and hands clutching her

chest as blood gushed through her fingers. A crimson stain spread out below her body.

Flute Girl screamed, "Mama!"

Ritchie stood up, and Flute Girl crawled across the floor to Peg's side, bawling. "Mama!"

Ritchie quickly secured the gun in his holster, grabbed his radio, and called for help.

Still shaking, I managed to get to my feet and stumble toward the kitchen. I passed the open basement door.

Still no Wesley.

I turned back to where Peg lay on the floor. Flute Girl's head was on Peg's chest, her mother's fresh blood shiny in her hair and on her face.

I ran into the kitchen and skidded to a stop. A smartphone in a black case with white polka dots sat on the counter. *My* smartphone. I snatched it up with a trembling hand.

Flute Girl's shrieking and wailing sent a chill down my back. I ran out the open kitchen door, down the steps, past Ritchie's patrol car, and down a patch of stiff, scratchy grass to the end of the driveway.

I stopped under the yard light.

The night was warm. Humid and still. Cicadas thrummed. I liked their sound. Comforting.

Outside. I was outside. The air was so fresh.

After a deep breath of that glorious air, I circled around to stare back at the house.

White.

Are you kidding me?

That house of horrors was painted *white*, with baby-blue shutters on the windows, where the glowing yellow light made the inside seem cozy. Normal.

I half expected the windows to be blacked out, the house itself some nasty run-down brick ranch, covered with noxious ivy. Would anyone believe this had been my prison? Or would they take a quick gander at this well-maintained bungalow and dismiss me with, *You made it all up?*

No, I didn't. It happened. They did it.

I hid behind a tree, out of the glow of the yard light, where I could see everything, but nobody could see me until I wanted them to. The mailbox was a few feet away, the address in reflective tape.

613 DAISY LANE.

Right.

I stayed there until sirens sliced into the rhythm of the cicadas.

I blinked.

First responders.

I blinked again.

For Peg.

Who was probably bleeding out that very minute.

The sirens wailed louder and louder. When the ambulance sped up the driveway, I followed it, sticking to the shadows.

A tall, heavyset man with a dark beard was the first out of the vehicle, wearing the same dark blue uniform as the small blond woman right on his heels. They ran into the house.

I couldn't make myself go inside, so I stood near the steps.

My phone vibrated. I touched the screen without thinking.

"Olivia?!" Mom's voice was high-pitched, loud.

"Please come get me."

"Oh my God, baby, where are you?"

"I don't know." Then I started to cry. Another police car pulled in, this one the county sheriff. A muscular older bald man in a dull green uniform with a serious gun belt strode over to me, jingling as he walked. His gaze lingered on my face, then drifted to my makeshift sling. He frowned. "Miss? Are you hurt?"

"Yes." My knees gave out. I collapsed into his arms just as everything went dark.

20

I WOKE UP in the back of an ambulance, lying on a gurney, my lower half tucked in tight under a white blanket. I took a deep breath.

Finally. Saved. "Hello?"

Someone was speaking up front, on the radio, and chatter came from outside through the gap in the open doors. There was an abbreviated whoop of a siren, not from my ambulance, though.

Another one?

I slid out of the bed and took a few wobbly steps to the back, where I grabbed the edge of one door and stuck my head out.

Flashing red and blue lights lit the night. An ambulance waited about fifty yards away behind the two law enforcement vehicles. Beside it, a gurney with a white-sheet-covered body.

Peg?

My knees threatened to give out, so I made my way back to the bed and lay down.

Was it really over?

Then the entire vehicle gave slightly as Officer Ritchie climbed in, stooping to avoid hitting his head on the roof.

I sat up.

He still looked like he was in pain from Flute Girl's punch.

"Is she—" My tone came across as sympathetic and kind, so I stopped. I wanted Peg to be dead. Didn't I?

He nodded once, slow.

"I didn't do it," I said.

"I know."

"Do they know? The sheriff? Does he know it wasn't me?"

He held up a hand. "Yes. They know. They know everything." He handed me my phone. "Sheriff says you dropped this out there."

I breathed out. "Thanks. And thank you for getting me out of there."

"If I had let you go the moment I saw you . . ." He trailed off and looked out the back of the ambulance. "It wouldn't have come to this." He sighed; there was a definite shakiness to the sound.

Did he blame himself for her death? He seemed broken up, but not like someone who had lost a loved one. More like someone who seemed equal parts sad and relieved. "I swear to you; I had just spent an hour trying to talk Peg into letting you go, telling her this whole revenge thing was pointless."

"Oh my God, what revenge? She kept going on and on about me apologizing for something, and I have no idea what it was. I know that we were at a novelist boot camp together, but whatever I said or did to her was a long time ago. I was fourteen!"

Neither of us said anything. Then his eyebrows rose. "We found Wesley locked in the basement. Claimed you attacked him with a knife."

I shook my head. "Not a knife. The edge of a box of waxed paper."

Ritchie's eyes widened. "Really?"

I nodded. "It's in my purse. Wherever that is. The rest of the wax paper box is in one of the tubs in the basement."

He tilted his head a little, almost a gesture of respect. "Resourceful."

"I worked with what I had."

"I should have gotten you out of there the minute I saw you." His gaze dropped to his feet.

"What will happen to Wesley?"

"He's been in trouble before. He did a little time in a court-ordered juvenile home last year for some Internet fraud."

"And Flu—" I swallowed. "Her daughter?"

He shrugged. "Psych evaluation for sure. After that, she has a father, somewhere. And Peg's parents may decide to become her guardians."

I shivered at the thought of Flute Girl out there running around. "She should be in therapy."

He nodded. "She'll get the care she needs."

"What happens to me?"

"The sheriff's office will question you. And you'll tell the truth. About everything that happened."

"I won't tell them about you seeing me before." I didn't know why; I guess I felt I owed him.

"Don't lie for me." He looked genuine. And sad. "I made a mistake."

So he did blame himself for Peg.

"You did the right thing in the end." I was quiet for a moment, thinking about the danger he'd been in when Flute Girl had the gun. His life had been on the line, too. "What if they don't believe me?"

"Peg's not . . . Peg wasn't crazy. She just went off the handle. People will believe your story. It wouldn't be a stretch to believe her capable of something like this. Especially given the backstory."

Was he talking about the boot camp?

Before I could ask, he handed me a slip of paper. "Here's my number if you have questions, or need anything."

Ritchie stayed there a moment, then his belt jangled as he went outside. The vehicle moved slightly as someone else came in, the blond lady who had run into the house earlier. "How you doing, sweetheart?"

"I'm out of there, at least," I said.

She studied my shoulder. "You in pain?"

I nodded. "I rolled my car on Friday. Been here ever since."

"Okay. We need to get you to Eugene for X-rays, but the ride could get bumpy. I'm going to give you an IV of fentanyl." She strapped on a pair of white plastic gloves. From a clear-fronted cabinet overhead that ran the length of the vehicle, she plucked out several white packets of different sizes.

"What is that?"

"Fentanyl?" She took my right hand. "Painkiller. Are you allergic to codeine or morphine?"

"I don't think so. Just bees."

She pulled down a narrow black jump seat from the side of the ambulance and sat down. First she cleaned the blood off my hand, then opened an alcohol packet and swabbed the back of my wrist. "Are you currently taking any medications?"

"No."

"Are you pregnant?"

I wanted to laugh, but didn't. "Um, no."

She opened up another packet and a silver needle flashed. I immediately dropped my head away from her and stared at the side of the ambulance. "Little poke here, sweetie."

A string of fire ran up the back of my hand. I scrunched my eyes shut.

"That slid right in. You okay?"

No words. I wasn't even in the vicinity of *okay*.

"Let me get this hooked up."

I opened my eyes and rolled my head back her way. She put some white tape on the back of my hand and attached a tube to the IV, then hung a plastic bag with clear fluid from a hook on the side of the ambulance. She twisted a little plastic switch on the tubing. "This may make you a little drowsy."

"Okay."

She set a hand on my leg. "The officer said your parents are already on their way."

"Good." I started to feel light-headed.

She watched me for a moment.

This was as it should have been, me getting help from someone nice who wanted to help me. Only it should have gone that way on Friday, right after I rolled my car.

Another reason to hate Peg. Even though she was dead.

A siren whooped, and I jumped.

The lady pressed down harder on my leg. "Just the other ambulance leaving."

So Peg was gone.

And they had Flute Girl.

And Wesley.

It was finally over.

They couldn't hurt me anymore.

The ambulance began to move. The rocking motion sent a jolt of pain up my shoulder, and I winced until the ride smoothed out. The ambulance accelerated. After a few minutes, my eyelids grew heavy.

I WOKE UP IN A HOSPITAL ROOM, MY LEFT ARM IN A PROPER BLACK sling, the throbbing pain that had dogged me for days finally gone. I was in a crisp, fresh-scented light blue hospital gown. The IV tube had disappeared; a bandage covered the back of my hand. I flexed my fingers. "Ow." The back of my hand felt bruised.

A plastic cup sat beside a yellow plastic pitcher on the little side table hanging over the edge of the bed. I picked up the cup and took a sip. Water. I drained it and shakily poured myself another glass. Gripping the pitcher hurt my hand and more spilled than made it in the cup. Still, I drank what did make it in. My stomach rumbled.

There were voices in the corridor. The door swung open, and my parents plunged into the room. "Oh, thank God, sweetie." Mom got to me first with a gentle hug, then Dad was at my side so he could kiss the top of my head.

"What happened?" asked Mom.

I shook my head. "Can we talk about something else?"

She glanced at Dad, and then nodded my way. "Of course, sweetheart. We talked to the doctor."

"What did he say?" I asked.

"She," said my dad. "You had a dislocated shoulder, some strained ligaments, a slight concussion."

"Anything else?" I rolled my eyes.

"Some bumps and bruises."

I could have diagnosed those. And I'd been right about the shoulder. Not to mention grateful that I wasn't awake when they put it back into place. "I want to go home."

"Later today, if you're up to it," said Dad.

I asked, "Can't we leave now?"

Mom set a hand on mine. "The police are waiting to talk to you when you're ready."

I groaned and rested my head against the back of the bed. "Can't it wait?"

"Better to get it over with." Mom sat on the edge of the

bed beside me. She didn't say anything else, and neither did Dad.

My stomach rumbled again.

Dad stood up. "I'll get you something to eat."

"Check with the nurse first; maybe she's on a restricted diet," said Mom.

"No." I spoke with more authority than ever before. "I haven't been sick; I've been kidnapped. I don't need special food."

Mom and Dad exchanged a look.

I sat up straight. "What?"

Tears filled Mom's eyes. "That's the thing. No one has told us anything. Other than that woman is dead." Mom shook her head. "Sweetie, what exactly happened?"

I took a deep breath. "The quick and dirty version? I rolled my car. That woman took me to her house and locked me in the basement. She kept me prisoner! She hurt me!"

Mom looked away. Dad put a hand on her shoulder but locked eyes with me. "Hurt you how?"

I shook my head. "Doesn't matter." I gestured at my shoulder. The psychological damage wasn't worth mentioning because it would just make me upset. "I'll be fine. But I don't care that she's dead! She deserved it!"

Mom forced a smile, leaned down toward the floor, then held out a Macy's bag. "Sweetie? I bought you some clothes to change into. And some toiletries."

Someone knocked on the door, and Dad went out into the

hall. He leaned back in. "The sheriff is here to do the questioning."

Mom asked, "After this can we take her home?"

Dad left for a second, then came back in and nodded.

"Thank God." I let out a big sigh and took the bag from my mom. "Can you leave so I can change?"

Mom nodded. "We'll be right outside. And they're letting us go out the back, so we can avoid the press."

"There's press?" I asked. "How'd they find out?"

"Social media. Someone in the hospital leaked it."

I pulled out black yoga pants and a long-sleeved red shirt, made of something incredibly soft. With shaking hands, I held them to my face and inhaled. New. Clean. Heaven.

There was also a white sports bra and underwear and a pair of black flip-flops. I ditched the hospital gown and dressed quickly. The clean clothes felt and smelled so good. I hoped to hell my others were gone forever.

I took the bag into the bathroom and stood in front of the mirror. I was really glad we were going to avoid the press because I still looked like crap.

The shadows under my eyes were gone. The little cuts and the scratch down my cheek had healed more, faded a bit. I found a brush and a package of hair ties, so I did my hair in a sloppy ponytail, best I could manage with one hand. *Almost back to normal.*

Last was a small bag of toiletries: deodorant, toothpaste, toothbrush, floss, some new Clinique mascara and gray eye shadow, and a chubby tube of lipstick in my favorite pink. I swiped that over my lips right after I brushed and flossed about nineteen times. I didn't bother with the rest of the makeup, and just tossed everything back in the bag.

I smiled at myself in the mirror. "Let's get this over with so I can see Rory."

21

THE SHERIFF HIMSELF came to my hospital room, and Mom stayed in there, more as a lawyer than a parent, it seemed. But he simply asked me to tell my story and interrupted me occasionally for details, all of which I provided, because I was telling the truth, after all. He didn't make me feel like a criminal because, of course, I wasn't one. The only omissions were when I peed my pants and when Wesley saw me naked in the window. He didn't ask me anything about Officer Ritchie, so I didn't offer.

I was torn about whether to call him out for seeing me and not helping. But I knew how evil Peg was. Maybe he had been a victim of hers as well. Something told me to let it go.

I could tell by the way the sheriff asked some of the same questions in different ways that he was looking for lies. But that's the thing about the truth: It gets told the same way each time. After an hour of questioning, my throat was sore from talking, and he seemed convinced I wasn't lying about any of it.

A nurse came in with a wheelchair. "Hospital policy."

I grabbed the Macy's bag and my phone off the bedside table. A piece of paper fluttered down. The nurse picked it up and handed it to me.

Ritchie's phone number. I shoved it in the bag.

Outside, my smile was ear to ear as I climbed in the passenger seat of my dad's SUV. Mom sat in the back. We stopped at a drive-through for a burger, fries, and a vanilla malt for me.

When we got to the house, several vehicles were at the end of the driveway. "Who is that?" I asked.

"Press," said Mom. "Get down."

I ducked below the windows until Dad got through the gates.

Inside, I went up to my room and tried to Skype Rory. No response.

I took a long bath, and then tried him again. Nothing.

Exhausted, I climbed into bed. But I couldn't sleep. Every time I shut my eyes, I had to snap them back open, to make sure I wasn't in a basement, trapped by a crazy woman.

I got back up and double-checked the locks on the windows, then opened up the curtains and let the moon shine in. I crawled back into bed and stared out at the night.

At some point, I finally nodded off.

When I awoke, I was afraid to open my eyes.

Could the last twenty-four hours have been a dream? Was I still in that basement? A prisoner?

I ran my hand over my left shoulder. Immobilized in a sling. A sling not made out of my cashmere sweater.

Slowly, I opened my eyes.

A white matelassé duvet covered me. Beyond my feet stood the hand-carved footboard of the madrone bed I'd special ordered from a local artist. I lifted my hand above my head and ran my fingers over the smooth headboard.

I sighed.

Home.

The sun streamed through the large window with the red-cushioned window seat. My gaze went over to my matching madrone dresser, my glass-topped writing desk, my two laptops, and expensive ergonomic office chair. The framed eight-by-ten enlargement of Rory's profile picture.

I breathed out. Everything would be fine. And as soon as I got in touch with Rory, everything would be perfect.

I slid out of bed and sat on the window seat, gazing out at the Cascade Mountains, which were still partially snow-topped from a heavier than normal snowfall and late arrival of spring.

I cranked open the window a bit. The day was sunny, in the seventies. A perfect day to be outside on the veranda and do nothing but relax. I used the bathroom, washed my face, and brushed my teeth. I'd barely changed into a pair of denim shorts and a black Oregon T-shirt when the doorbell rang.

"Olivia!" yelled my mom.

Downstairs, I walked into our massive kitchen. My agent, Billy, was seated on a high stool at the island, in his usual three-piece suit and tie, with black horn-rimmed glasses bordering on geek, yet chic.

"Billy!"

He lifted his hands in the air, and in his loud British accent exclaimed, "There's my girl!"

I grinned and stepped into his arms.

"I am so sorry I couldn't get here before now." He squeezed me for a solid minute before letting me go. He set a hand on either side of my face, and his forehead wrinkled. "I don't even think we want to cover that up."

"Cover what up?" I climbed up onto the stool next to him.

He took a sip from the tumbler of iced tea in front of him. "Your face."

"Oh, thanks." I rolled my eyes, a little bit insulted.

Billy laughed. "No, my dear, not what I meant. Your war wounds. We don't want to cover them up." He glanced at his watch. "Speaking of, we'd better get ready."

"Ready for what?" I asked.

Billy smiled. "An interview for the *Today* show."

"Oh my God." I put my hand to my mouth. "Are you serious?"

Mom laughed.

"You knew?" I glanced from her to Billy.

Mom nodded. "The *Today* show! Can you believe it?"

Did I really want anyone to see me? "I'm not ready."

"You need to do this." Mom looked over at Billy. "We thought it would be better than waiting."

Billy said, "There is already so much speculation, especially with that woman dead. Better to get your side of the story out there."

As much as I didn't want to do the interview, they were right. I wiped my eyes and slid off the chair, landing on the cool, tile floor in my bare feet. "I need to change. How much time do we have?"

Billy said, "About forty-five minutes. They happened to have one of their feature reporters in Portland, and she's on her way."

"What should I wear? What should I say?" I didn't even know where to start.

"First, calm down. You're recovering from a terrible ordeal. And you have nothing to hide. You are the victim, no matter what happened to that woman. She was in the wrong, and you are confident because you have the truth on your side. No need for pretense. So keep it simple and casual."

I climbed back up on the stool.

He glanced at my shorts and shirt. "Less casual than that."

I rolled my eyes and got back down.

He smiled. "And you'll just answer her questions with candor and honesty. Be yourself. Because the public will love who you are: a teenager who survived a nightmare situation."

"What, and then they'll want to run out and buy my books?"

He pointed up. "From your lips to God's ear."

I touched my hair. "And what about—"

"Something soft that makes you look young. Vulnerable. We want as much sympathy as possible." His words bubbled out. "And tears are good! Don't worry if you start to cry."

"I'd hate to see how happy you'd be if I really got hurt."

"Oh, stop." Billy patted my hand. "We need to make the most of the attention. That's all."

Mom said, "I could French braid your hair."

I didn't want my hair like that ever again. "Just a ponytail maybe."

"I'll tell them to go light on the makeup," said Billy.

Upstairs I took a shower; then Mom dried my hair and put it back in a low ponytail. I dressed in jeans, flip-flops, and a white linen sleeveless button-down. I chose a pair of silver hoop earrings and looked at myself in the mirror. Definitely almost back to normal.

When I returned downstairs, a cameraman was setting up out on the veranda, which afforded the same fabulous view of Mount Bachelor as out my window. A thin blond woman in a gray sheath dress and high black pumps held out her hand to me. "I'm Lucy Voss, NBC News."

She looked familiar as I shook her hand. "I feel under-dressed."

Ms. Voss smiled. "Oh, don't feel that way. You look great, Olivia." She beckoned to another woman, who had long dark hair and purple lipstick and wore a flimsy black tank dress and black combat boots. "Delilah, she's ready."

Delilah patted the chair in front of her. "Over here."

I sat down, and she rubbed something nice-smelling into my skin. Her eyes were brown, golden circles bordering the pupils. She said, "We won't do a whole makeover or anything. Your agent wants people to see the truth."

"The truth?"

Delilah nodded. "You've been through something, and you came out the other side. Let the public see what bravery costs."

Bravery? "I guess I hadn't thought of myself as brave."

She smiled. "Maybe you should start."

Delilah plucked my brows a bit, then added a touch of mascara, and put something on my lips. She stepped back and frowned, then relaxed. "Good to go."

The cameraman took a little more time to get the lighting right before he waved me over. I sank into a cushy green chair, Lucy Voss opposite me. She leaned in, fastened a microphone to the collar of my shirt, and said, "Since we're taping this and have time to edit, I'd rather just ask you questions and have your reactions, instead of prepping you."

I glanced over at Billy. He was on his phone, but gave me a thumbs-up.

I nodded.

My parents were a few feet away off camera. Dad wore a frown and had his arms crossed, but Mom was grinning. Delilah had disappeared. It was just me and the reporter, plus the camera guy hidden behind his equipment. "I'm ready," I said.

"Great. I will make an intro segment that tells the basic story, based on the sheriff's report, so America will know what happened. But we want you to fill us in on how you felt during the ordeal."

I nodded.

Lucy Voss and the cameraman conferred a bit. Then the camera was rolling, the lights were bright in my eyes, and she asked her first question. "Livvy, America has been captivated by your story, from the first reports that you were missing until you were found. You're a well-known, bestselling author. This is almost like a Stephen King novel come to life. Tell us, how are you feeling today?"

I smiled and gestured at my shoulder. "Other than having to wear this sling, I'm feeling pretty good."

"Excellent," said the reporter. "Can you tell us when you knew you were in trouble?"

In trouble? "Um, I guess when my car flipped. I knew my shoulder was hurt, and I maybe had a concussion. I knew that I needed help. But . . ." Would America believe me if I told them about Flute Girl? "I guess the worst moment was waking up in that basement. I was in bad shape and didn't know where I was."

"And that's when the woman took you captive?" Her voice held a tad too much enthusiasm for me.

"I guess so. I mean, I was already captive. That was just when I realized that help wasn't coming, and she wasn't letting me go. I realized that I was on my own." A stray piece of hair fell into my eyes. I swiped it away.

"So you had no idea why the woman might have wanted to keep you there as her prisoner?"

I shook my head.

My mom was still grinning; my dad just looked nervous.

The reporter continued, "So, at the time, you had no idea who she was."

Why was she dwelling on that? My tone held a tinge of snark when I parroted her line. "No, i had no idea who she was."

Lucy Voss reached behind her and picked up a box of waxed paper.

Did she have that there the whole time?

She handed it to me. "Do you mind showing us what you did to escape that horrible basement?"

"Yeah, I guess." I stuck the waxed paper between my legs. My hand was shaking a little, but I managed to tear off the cutting edge. I bent the metal back and forth, separating it into two pieces, just like I did in the basement. I held up the piece to the camera.

Ms. Voss took it from me. "May I say that this is the most ingenious weapon?" She started to touch it to her own hand.

"Careful, that's kinda sh—"

She exclaimed a bit as she drew blood. "Oh, that's sharp."

What a dolt. "Yeah."

She set the thing down and continued, "What did you do with this?"

I swallowed. I didn't exactly want to go in to the part where I let Wesley stick his tongue down my throat. "She had a cousin, this guy. He came into the basement when she wasn't home. I cut him with that, surprised him, and then I ran out and locked the door."

Lucy Voss nodded a few times. "Can you tell us what happened after you got out of the basement?"

"I went upstairs and tried to get out of the house." My

heartbeat sped up. Just talking about it brought it all back. I was beginning to wonder if this interview was a good idea.

She frowned, but not like a real, ugly frown. More like a pensive, thoughtful one that didn't detract from her looks. I wondered how long she'd practiced that in the mirror. "Was there someone else in the house you encountered?"

I nodded. "The daughter of the woman."

"Did you have to attack the daughter as well?"

I vehemently shook my head. Telling America I beat up a kid would not help my sales whatsoever; I knew that, even though she was the one who killed her mother. "I . . . I was able to get her in the basement stairway and lock her in as well." I swallowed. "She wasn't hurt." I couldn't exactly say the same for her flute.

Lucy Voss shook her head. "So amazing you were able to escape on your own, with your injury." She glanced at her notes. "And then the woman, known only to you as Peg, came home."

I nodded, but didn't say anything.

Lucy Voss prompted me. "What happened then?"

I hesitated. Did I want America to know what I had done? Hell, they already had the news version. They might as well get the actual truth. "I took a knife from the kitchen and planned to defend myself." I straightened up in my chair and lifted my chin. "I just wanted to get home."

"And then a state patrolman was alerted to your situation, and the woman was shot with his weapon during a struggle, correct?"

"But he didn't shoot her." I didn't know how many details were out. I wished I had asked. "The girl got the gun."

"Yes, we're aware of that." The reporter looked at her notes and seemed to pause before asking, "And now that you know who she is, does that change things? Knowing that perhaps this was on her agenda all along?"

I frowned and glanced over at Billy. Did they know about the novelist boot camp? That Peg and I had crossed paths before? He didn't look shocked. I shook my head and decided to play dumb. "I don't know what you mean by that."

The reporter said, "Peg, as you call her, is Judith Margaret Cutler. You weren't aware of that?"

Judith Margaret Cutler. Something about it seemed familiar. But why should that mean anything to me? I shook my head. "I don't know what . . ."

My words faded as Lucy Voss held up a paperback copy of *The Quest for the Coven.*

My mouth dropped open.

"J. M. Cutler is the author of this young adult novel, which was published about six months after Livvy's own novel, *The Caul and the Coven.*"

I gripped the edge of the chair with my one good hand. "What the hell?" My heartbeat throttled up. I had been worried about my side of the story, that people might feel sorry for Peg since she was dead. And I could only imagine what Peg considered to be her side of the whole story. She'd been vilified on the Internet, thanks to my fans. Whether she was guilty of plagiarism or not. But this revelation meant that I was on even more solid footing where my side of the story was concerned. Not only had Peg been aware of who I was, she held a long-standing grudge against me. "Billy? Did you know this?"

The reporter rolled her eyes and did a slashing motion across her throat. "We'll cut that. Let's go back."

"No." I didn't want the country to see my reaction to the discovery that not only had my abductor caused me bodily harm and mental anguish over the past few days, but she had caused me considerable stress when her book came out long before this all happened. Lucy Voss was not getting her freaking scoop. Not from me, anyway. "No way. I'm done." I tore the microphone off my shirt and threw it at her feet. "This interview is *over*." I flung myself out of the chair. "Billy! When did you find out?!" I stomped over to where he was pretending to be busy on his phone. "Billy!"

He sighed and met my gaze. "Yes. I was recently made aware and—"

"And you didn't bother to tell me?" I waved a hand at the reporter. "You set this all up knowing that she'd tell me who Peg was? How could you do that?"

Billy said, "Don't you see? This isn't just a random crazy person."

Mom added, "This makes it a real story, sweetie."

"It's not a story! It's my life!" The tears had finally arrived in the form of a knot in my throat. "I'm not doing this, not now. And I don't want any of that airing."

Dad took my arm.

Lucy Voss had come up behind me. "We can continue whenever you're ready."

I shook my head. "I'm done." Then I ran inside, up the stairs to my room, and slammed the door. Then, only then, did I let the tears come.

22

FIRST MOM CAME knocking on my door, then Dad, then Billy. I refused to open it for any of them. Then Lucy Voss actually tried. "Olivia, we can do this interview your way. We don't have to talk about J. M. Cutler if you don't want to."

I snapped up my middle finger and shoved it in the air at the door. "Go away," I whispered.

Finally, she did.

There was only one person I wanted to talk to. Only one person I wanted to see. Rory. I picked up the frame with his photo and kissed it. Then I turned on my laptop and Skype and clicked on the photo of Rory and VIDEO CALL. The thing beeped, but I quickly cut it off.

No. I didn't want to Skype.

That wasn't good enough. Not nearly. I deserved more. I wanted to see Rory in person. Face to face. I wanted to cry on his shoulder about this whole episode, not slobber on my laptop while he watched from across the country.

I stayed in my room until I was pretty sure everyone had left, and then I opened my door and listened. Mom and Dad were talking in the kitchen, but I heard no one else. I tiptoed down the stairs and stood by the kitchen door. Definitely only them. I stepped inside. "Where's Billy?"

They stopped talking. Mom said, "I had no idea about any of that. About that *woman* being that *plagiarist*."

I asked again, "Where's Billy?"

Dad said, "Hotel. He wants to come see you later."

I rolled my eyes. "Well, he can wait."

"Sweetie, are you hungry?" asked Mom.

I shook my head. "I want to go to Chicago."

Dad frowned.

Mom shook her head. "You just got back, you're still recovering. We could take a vacation next week maybe—"

"It's not a vacation," I said. "I want to see my boyfriend."

Mom and Dad exchanged a glance. She said, "That boy you've been Skyping with?"

I nodded. "Yes, but he's not just the boy I've been Skyping with. I love him, and he loves me. I want to see him in person. I'm tired of waiting."

Mom said, "You're not going alone. I'll book flights for us."

I threw my hand up. "Fine. I don't care if you go with me. I just want to go. And I *am* going."

Dad scratched his chin. "What do you even know about this boy?"

"Everything," I said. "He's my age; he's in a million AP classes." I sighed. "He's a good guy, Dad. Trust me."

The corner of his lips turned up. "So where in Chicago does he live?"

I bit my bottom lip. "I'm not exactly sure. We've only Skyped."

Mom and Dad exchanged another look.

"Don't do that!" I yelled. "Why can't you just help me find him? I just want to go there and surprise him."

"We'll help," Mom said. "I'm sure Billy's got people who can—"

"No!"

They both looked at me.

"This is personal! I don't want Billy involved, or it'll end up on the news."

Dad said, "I'll do it."

I sighed. "Thanks, Dad."

He walked over to the phone for the pad of paper there, then grabbed a pen and clicked it. "Go. What's this boy's name?"

"Rory." I smiled. "Rory Calhoun."

Dad laughed. "Okay. But seriously."

I frowned. "I am serious."

Dad glanced at Mom.

"Stop it!" I yelled. "Stop exchanging these stupid glances like I'm an idiot."

"Sweetie," said Dad. "You're not an idiot. It just struck me as funny, because Rory Calhoun was in movies back in the fifties. Your grandmother had a huge crush on him."

"Oh," I said. "Well maybe Rory's mother was a fan or something."

"Maybe," said Mom. "What are his parents' names?"

I shrugged. "We don't talk about his parents."

Dad wrote the name down. "So we have a name, no neighborhood or parents. What about school?"

I shook my head. "I don't know."

Mom and Dad looked at each other.

I slammed my hand on the counter. "Stop it!"

Mom said, "You just don't seem to know very much about this boy."

"I know what I need to know! He is a great listener, and he's there for me, and we have a lot in common, and he loves me! Those are the things that matter! The rest is just details, for God's sake!" I took a breath and sat down on a stool. "Please, just help me find him."

Dad nodded. "We will. Okay? We will. But it may take a day or so. Okay?"

I breathed out. "Okay."

Mom said, "Just take some time. Relax while your dad figures it out. Can you do that?"

I nodded.

"Now, are you hungry?" she asked.

I nodded. "Starved."

After a lunch of Cobb salad and a mint Skinny Cow ice cream sandwich, I retreated to my room. I wanted to tell Mom and Dad I'd decided to put off college, at least for the time being. But since I already had them on edge about Rory—not to mention the whole *Today* show/J. M. Cutler fiasco—I figured it would be better to wait on that part.

And there was something else I wanted to know more about. What happened at boot camp that made Peg hate me?

I went into my closet and dug out a box of papers. I tended to lack organizational skills, and sort of just shoved everything together. There was no chance of anything getting lost that way because I knew exactly where it was, but putting my finger on a specific paper was tough. With my one good hand, I dragged the box out of the closet and over to my bed. I sat down on the carpet, my back against the bed, and began to pull stuff out. The first pile of paper was a draft of *The Caul and the Coven.*

I began to skim it.

I remembered when I began the story. Mom and I were on the flight home from the novelist boot camp in Los Angeles. I was excited as well as anxious. I knew I wanted to start writing, but I was so scared about what would happen if I didn't succeed. But, of course, the excitement overcame the anxiety, and I started writing an idea that popped into my head.

By the time we landed at the airport in Redmond, just north of Bend, I had a brief outline written.

I set that draft on the floor and pulled out another manuscript. It took me six months of revisions to get the story right. And then another month for Billy to agree to represent me. I set that manuscript aside, as well as the next two I dug out. And then, there it was: the red folder like Peg's.

I hadn't looked at it for years.

I set it in my lap and opened it up. The photograph was at the top, and I put that aside without looking at it. Next were the marked-up pages of my manuscript critiqued by the other participants. I scanned my story. God, it was so lame. Some dumb thing I'd submitted about a boy falling in love with a girl vampire. I had tried to put a spin on *Twilight*, switch the roles. I shook my head as I paged through the seven copies of it, the ones the other participants had written on. How had I gone from something so stupid to something so brilliant in a matter of hours? I mean, my idea for *The Caul and the Coven* was so commercial and so *right*.

Fate, I guessed. I was meant to write that story.

I stared at my toes for a moment. When did the exact idea strike me? We were seated in first class on the flight home, I knew that. Mom had a glass of wine, I had a ginger ale, and we shared a boxed meal of crackers and cheese and dried fruit. I shrugged.

Well, it had been nearly four years.

I paged through a few more of my manuscript pages and stopped. A note in my handwriting was on someone else's manuscript page. Weird, because I gave all the other people their manuscripts back. My note read: *Make this into twin sisters (maybe living in Portland?) and have the mother be trapped in books instead of jewelry? Could be sooooo cool . . .*

I quickly skimmed the pages. Twins, a boy and a girl, live with their grandmother in Salem, Massachusetts. In the attic, they discover their mother trapped inside a pendant and decide to go on a journey to collect the matching pendants in order to set her free. At the end of the pages was a note from the author: *Thanks so much for reading my pages! I hope you liked them.* ☺ *JMC*

JMC. Judith Margaret Cutler?

I froze. Peg.

I had gotten my inspiration from her manuscript. I had forgotten her, but she had remembered me. And she knew I'd taken her idea, not the other way around.

The papers fell out of my hand, drifting to the floor.

I'd taken Peg's idea, changed a few things, and made it my own. Was it close enough to Peg's to be stealing? Would anyone think that?

I grabbed my laptop off my bed and went to Goodreads, quickly typing in *The Quest for the Coven by J. M. Cutler.*

I scrolled down the reviews. Most had two stars, maybe three, no real love for the book. I sucked in my breath. Someone had written: *Such a total rip-off of The Caul and the Coven. All she did was change a few things. Livvy Flynn should file a lawsuit.*

My heart pounded. "Holy crap." No wonder Peg was pissed at me. I had turned Peg's idea into a worldwide success.

I shook my head. No. *No!*

One of the first things I learned about publishing was that beginning writers always wondered whether they should get a copyright before they sent their stories in to publishers. But ideas can't be copyrighted. A girl falls in love with a vampire. Anyone in the world could write a story with that premise.

Peg's idea: A brother and sister go looking for their lost mother, who is trapped inside an object.

I shook my head. I didn't do anything wrong.

So maybe Peg's story excerpt had given me an idea, but how

much was in those few pages? Certainly not the whole three-book series. Other than the basic premise of two children going on a quest to free their mother, the rest was all from my imagination: all the subplots and romances and dangerous creatures. I had made up the other 99.9 percent of the story; anyone with a brain would agree with that.

Plus, my book had come out before Peg's. So the only people who knew would be me and Peg and . . . the other people in our critique group at the boot camp. But would they remember? I couldn't recall a single premise of anyone else's story. I hadn't even remembered Peg's.

And writing was so self-centered: Everyone would have left there the same way I had, ready to start my own story, not giving a crap about anyone I had just met.

Was anyone at that workshop aware of my success? Unless they lived under a rock, yes. If anyone had suspected anything, drawn the conclusion about the similarities between the stories, wouldn't they have come forward? Peg herself hadn't even come forward.

I sighed. I no longer had to wonder why Peg had it in for me. And that day when she'd shoved me in the bathroom and Ritchie had found me, Peg had said something like, "This is the one I told you about."

So Ritchie knew. That was what he meant by backstory.

What happened if this came out?

Would people think she had a good enough reason for kidnapping me? Would they think I deserved it?

Would everyone think I stole her story?

I sucked in a breath.

But Peg was dead.

And my secret was safe.

Still, after a few moments, I made a phone call to a number I never planned to dial.

"Ritchie, here."

"This is Livvy Flynn."

A slight pause. "What can I do for you?"

"I didn't say anything to the sheriff about seeing you in the basement."

"I appreciate that."

I swallowed. "I don't know what you know about me. And Peg. About when we were at the novelist boot camp in LA."

"I heard her side of it."

I said, "I didn't remember until now, but her story idea led me to the inspiration for mine. But I didn't steal her story."

"I think she knew that. But she had such a hard time. . . . Tell me, what happened when you wrote your first book?"

I stumbled on my words a bit. "Well, I got an agent, and he sold it at auction—"

"*At auction*. You say it like it's a given. What happened next?"

I wanted to hang up. But I didn't. He knew my secret. "Well, I went on a tour with my mom and a publicist."

"Again with the givens. Seriously? Let me ask: How much did you get for that first book?"

"The first book or the series?"

"Whichever."

I wasn't going to tell him I got a hundred and fifty thousand for the three books. *Each*. "About six figures."

"You know what Peg got for her novel? Go ahead, guess."

I didn't want to.

"Go ahead. Guess."

I knew my book deal had been good, better than good. So I tried to guess what a fairly low advance would be. "Um, thirty thousand?"

Ritchie said, "Try ten thousand. And Peg was thrilled. It was her dream come true, to have a book published. She sold her novel three months before you sold yours. To an imprint at your publisher. Did you know that?"

I had no idea. No one ever told me. Maybe that was another reason why Billy had been dead set against a lawsuit. "No."

"But the news about your deal was everywhere. And apparently, when everyone responded so hugely to the amazing story of a teenage author, Peg's book—considered to be sort of similar to yours—got put on a back burner. Her editor told her they were delaying it for a year or two, to let yours get out there first, and then hers could jump on the coattails."

I could imagine, like all those *If you loved* The Hunger Games, *you'll love this*. I knew what he would say next and preempted him. "But then all the fans of my book accused her of copying me."

"They were pretty brutal to her online. You know how she celebrated her book coming out, before all the crap started?

"No."

"A signing at our local library. Three people came. I was one of them."

I thought about the book launch my publisher had thrown at Books of Wonder in New York City. Mom had gone to a Starbucks to get ice for my wrist after all the autographs. "I thought, I just thought . . . I thought everyone got a book tour and a lot of money and . . ."

He said nothing for a moment. "After I saw you in the basement, Peg explained why she did it. Why she took you. She said it all happened so fast. When the kid ran into the house to tell her about the car accident, she grabbed her phone to call 911. But the kid has made up stories before, so she went to make sure she was telling the truth. But when she saw the personalized license plate lying in the road, she knew it was you."

"But why?"

Ritchie didn't answer right away. "Peg knew you didn't steal her story, at least not in a way she could prove, and even then it was subjective. There was no way for her to ever show that your entire series came from what you saw at boot camp. But she wanted to try to prove you had stolen it from her. And she thought that maybe if you—"

"Stayed in the basement long enough I'd confess to something I didn't even do?" I shook my head. "But I didn't. Because I didn't do anything other than get an idea from someone else. Happens all the time."

Ritchie said, "I know Peg. *Knew* Peg." Silence for a moment.

"I think when she saw you there, in your car, she lost it. She thought, here's my chance, my chance to make her pay for taking away the dream."

"It was my dream, too. Why couldn't I have my dream?"

"Peg was obsessed with you. Read about you on the Internet. She hated that you seemed so . . . entitled. Like just because you wrote a book, then you should automatically get everything else that goes with it: fame, money, success. I think she was mad that you had no idea that tons of people have books come out every year and never have any of that."

I didn't say anything for a moment. "Are you going to tell people about this?"

"Not my place. And I think you've suffered enough."

I breathed out. "I have to go. And . . . I am sorry about Peg."

He was quiet for a moment. "Me too." He hung up.

I went downstairs. Dad and Mom stopped talking the moment I stepped in the room.

"What are you talking about?"

Mom pointed to my carry-on. "Lane County Sheriff's Office dropped off your stuff."

I sat down. "That wasn't what you were talking about."

Dad looked at Mom, then back at me. "Liv, I did some checking on the boy in Chicago."

"Can you please call him Rory?"

"Listen, Liv. I had my tech guy trace his Skype. Which was not entirely legal, I'm sure. But—"

"You found him?" I smiled.

"You're sure he's in Chicago?"

203

I dropped into a chair across from him. "Of course he's in Chicago. Why would you ask that?"

"He can't be. At least, he's not Skyping from there. His IP didn't trace to Chicago."

"What does that mean?" I asked.

"For one thing, it means he hasn't been completely honest with you. Maybe you don't know him as well as you thought. Or . . ."

"Or what?"

"Or someone was messing with you all along. Sweetheart, we need you to consider the possibility that Rory may be fake."

I shook my head. "He is real. He *is* real." Déjà vu. I felt like I'd already had this conversation.

I gasped. I had. With Wesley.

I jumped to my feet and grabbed my carry-on, knocking it to its side. I squatted beside it and quickly unzipped.

The clothes were neatly folded. If the police had searched it, they'd put everything back where they'd found it. I stuck my hand down at the bottom, feeling for the secret compartment with the hidden zipper. I found it and unzipped.

I stuck my hand in, expecting to find it empty. But my fingers closed around the thick black leather book. The red ribbon still marked the last page I'd written nearly a week ago. It seemed untouched.

As though no one had found it.

I shut the journal.

My secrets were still secret.

But then how did Peg know those things about me? The hair pulling? And how did Wesley know the things he said about Rory? He knew exactly when we Skyped. *He quoted me the line that Rory always used to sign off, for God's sake.* I walked back to the table. "What's the address?"

"I don't see how this will help—"

"Dad! Tell me the address!"

He slid the piece of paper over just as I heard a familiar beep from upstairs. Skype.

"That's him! That's Rory now!"

Without looking at it, I crumpled the address in my hand as I tore up the stairs, wincing when I brushed my arm against the banister. I ran down the hall to my room. My laptop was on my bed, and I quickly clicked ANSWER WITH VIDEO.

"Rory?"

Silence. The familiar black square sat in the middle of the screen.

"Rory? You there? Can you see me? I've missed you so much. I'm coming to see you!"

And then it flickered.

Did he get his camera fixed? Was I finally going to get to see him and prove everyone wrong?

"Rory, I'm so glad—"

My words dropped away as a person appeared on the screen.

An unsmiling Wesley.

"No. No no no no." I shook my head as tears filled my eyes. My hands trembled. I glanced down at the crumpled paper in my hand and unfolded it.

613 Daisy Lane. Nimrod, Oregon.

Peg's address.

My stomach clenched, and suddenly I couldn't breathe.

That was why he sounded familiar.

I clapped my hand over my mouth.

Nooooooooooo.

I *loved* Rory. And he loved *me*.

He thought I was beautiful. He told me so.

I covered my face with my hands.

But it was all fake. Rory was merely Wesley pretending, toying with me, telling me what I wanted to hear. That meant . . .

He didn't love me.

He didn't think I was beautiful.

And I was terrified that no one ever would.

I lowered my hands. Wesley was still there.

My skin crawled at the sight of him, but I had to know. "Why aren't you in jail?"

"For what? Peg was crazy. And they found me locked in the basement, bleeding. I cooperated completely."

"Why did you help her?"

"Peg was obsessed with you. She offered to pay me to hack into your e-mail and Facebook, but I had already gotten in trouble for that. So then I came up with a better idea. Create someone you trusted and would talk to. Maybe spill some secrets to." He sounded proud.

"Rory." The name caught in my throat. *Don't cry, don't cry.*

He nodded. "And I had to babysit for Peg every Sunday

anyway, so I brought my laptop and did the Skypes at her house."

So much made sense. Flute Girl hated me on sight because she already hated me. She had some weird kind of crush on her cousin and must have known he Skyped with me. Maybe she hated that he sent her to bed so that he could spend time with me.

But I didn't want it to make sense! I didn't want this, the lie, to be the truth.

There had to be something—anything—that would make it not be true. "But I have his picture." I hated the tinge of whine in my voice.

"I got it off an online yearbook in the Bay Area. The rest is fake. Got the name from an old movie on television."

Dad was right.

My throat got thick. I swallowed, trying to hold off the sobs.

Wesley shook his head. "When I found out you were in Peg's basement . . ."

I tried to keep my voice steady. "Did you ever think about calling the police?"

He looked off in the distance for a moment. "I owed Peg a lot. She paid for my lawyer when I got in trouble before." He sighed. "Blood is blood, man."

I disconnected and began to cry.

Rory wasn't real. He didn't love me. He didn't think I was beautiful.

That was the truth. Whether it scared me or not, I had to face it.

I heaved the picture frame against the wall, glass tinkling as it fell. I carefully extracted the picture and ripped Rory into pieces that drifted to the floor.

Then I deleted my Skype.

I'd been so wrong.

Peg could still hurt me.

I bawled and pounded my fist on the desk.

I hated her.

Eventually, the tears stopped. I sniffled and wiped my eyes.

But did the blame lie completely with her?

With Wesley?

They set the trap.

But it wouldn't have worked without me.

Why had I been so willing to start an online relationship when I had barely talked to a boy in real life since middle school?

I went into the bathroom for a box of tissues.

Other girls would have had a boyfriend, or at least someone they liked. Chances are, they would have blown off a guy on the Internet because they had real people in their lives.

But I had no one. No friends. Certainly no boyfriend.

Rory was exactly what I wanted. Someone who said exactly what I wanted to hear. I only had to deal with him on Sunday nights; I was always in control.

Rory had been perfect for someone like me because, truthfully, there was something that scared me even more than finding out Rory wasn't real and didn't love me or think I was beautiful.

My ultimate fear—which was probably a holdover from all those years of being a victim—lay in granting someone real the power to love me or *not*, think me beautiful or *not*.

Handing someone the capacity to hurt me was the real terror.

And that was why Wesley and Peg hit pay dirt.

Anyone else would have been skeptical, blown it off in favor of the real people in their lives.

I was such an easy target, dying for an easy relationship because I didn't want the inconvenience of a real person who might not do things as I wanted him to.

If I stayed at home, I would remain that target. Always wanting a relationship that couldn't hurt me. Someone else could just as easily dupe me again because I hadn't learned a thing.

That couldn't happen.

As scary as it was, I had to put myself back into real life.

Eventually, I had to get out. I had to go to college.

There was no good reason to continue being afraid to put myself out there. I had survived not only Peg, but my childhood. There was also no good reason to keep feeling guilty about coming through the other side in basically one piece.

Peg didn't die by my hand, but ultimately, her demise had something to do with me. My actions contributed.

But I had paid for that, hadn't I?

First, by my time in her basement.

And second, with Rory.

There was no need for me to feel guilty.

I would have scars forever because of Peg.

But that woman had brought it on herself. She could have called 911 when they found me. She could have made sure I was safe, then confronted me about everything.

But she didn't.

And she was dead.

And Flute Girl was motherless.

None of that was my fault.

Which left only one thing I should feel bad about. And there was an easy way to get that off my mind.

I blew my nose, then picked up my phone and called Billy.

He answered on the first ring. "Yes?"

"I'll do the interview under one condition."

Billy's words were quick and loud. "What? Anything!"

"Got a pen?" I picked up the scrap of paper with Peg's address on it and dictated.

"Liv, what do you want me to do?"

"I need you to send a new flute there. The best money can buy." Then I clicked END and tossed the phone on the bed.

"There. Done. Now move on."

Epilogue

IT'S A SATURDAY afternoon in January, halfway through my second week of college. Mom and Dad agreed to let me reapply for the winter term. I did the *Today* show interview but didn't tell all, in case I do decide to write a book about it. And then I spent the rest of the summer finishing the third novel of my series and the fall on my last tour for a while.

My hope was to start up another series right after that, so I could stay home a while longer. But I sat for the better part of a week, staring at the blank screen of my computer.

Tons of ideas floated around in my head, and I started several times, but nothing stuck. There seemed to be no point in putting off school any longer.

I had no more excuses for staying out of the real world.

So after the first of the year, I packed up my black Honda Civic with no vanity plates—I felt the need for a less flashy replacement—and headed to Eugene.

I don't know when—if—I'll start another novel. I kind of like school, my classes. I'm surprised that I do, considering I haven't been in a classroom since eighth grade. I'm still not putting myself out there much. Maybe I'm waiting to find someone who has something in common with me. I seem to be the only one on my floor actually from Oregon. This place is like Cal State Eugene.

But I guess it's enough that I'm here, someplace other than home.

Small steps.

I'm in the dorm lounge, a space of plush chairs and couches in bright colors. Everyone else is at the basketball game, which is why I actually came out of my room.

Groups of students still get my heart pounding. I want to belong, but it's so much easier to not try. Also safer.

I'm on a couch, reading "The Pit and the Pendulum" for a class.

"Livvy?"

I look up and see a girl from down the hall. I stifle a groan. Her mailbox is next to mine. Once when we got our mail at the same time, she recognized my name on an envelope, and now she won't leave me alone. I avoid her whenever possible, but now she has me trapped.

She smiles and hands me an envelope. "Got this in my mail by mistake."

"Thanks." Without looking at it, I set it beside me on the couch. *Go away.*

She waits a moment, for what I'm not sure.

I hold up my book. "I've got a test Monday."

"Well, see you later." She leaves and I go back to reading.

A deep voice says, "Not my favorite of Poe's."

My heart stops.

Standing in front of me is a dark-haired, blue-eyed guy, dressed in jeans and a green T-shirt with a yellow O.

Rory.

I swallow.

Obviously *not* the fake Rory invented by Wesley. But this non-Rory looks so much like that picture I ripped up so many months ago that I can't breathe.

"Didn't mean to startle you."

On second thought, he doesn't look as much like Rory as I thought. Maybe that picture has dulled in my mind, but this guy's jaw seems more square, his eyes a darker blue. Plus, the guy standing in front of me is *real*.

"I recognize you from class." He points at the literature textbook on the cushion next to me.

He's in my class? How have I never seen him?

Because I sit in the front row and never look around.

Despite my big plans for taking control of my life, I am still hiding and shy. My chance to start fresh is staring me in the face, and I am letting it slip by.

Grow some, Livvy.

Grab on to life and start living.

I smile. Holy crap, what did one even say to an actual living, breathing guy who isn't separated from me by half a country and a nonfunctioning webcam?

What do you say to someone you want to get to know?

I have no clue.

And what comes out of my mouth is something I've been thinking for days but haven't had the nerve to say to anyone. "So our prof sure likes to listen to himself talk."

"Right?" He picks up the envelope and my textbook and plops down beside me. "It's like, *Shut up already, dude.*" He grins, revealing dimples, and then sticks out his hand. "I'm Nick."

His warm, strong hand around mine sends a shiver straight up my arm. Yet I manage to say, in a somewhat normal tone of voice, "Livvy. And I'm really glad to meet you."

I'm disappointed when he releases my hand, but then he says, "Pretty quiet around here today. Want to go to dinner later? Hear they're making that mac and cheese with the bread crumbs on top."

"Okay." A rush of heat runs up my neck.

"Meet here at five?"

I nod, unable to speak.

"Cool." He gets to his feet, and the envelope flutters to the floor. He hands it to me. "See you later."

I smile and watch him go, my heart pounding. I glance at the envelope. My name and address are typed, and there's no return address. I open it and pull out a folded sheet of paper. Something falls to the floor.

I lean over to look.

Next to my foot is a dead wasp.

I kick it away and scream, then slap a hand over my mouth. I grab my books and run back to my room. I realize I haven't looked at the paper. I sink down on my bed. My hands are shaking so bad that I have trouble unfolding it at first.

There, in childish handwriting, someone has scrawled:

Buzz. Buzz. Buzz.

I crumple up the paper and throw it to the other side of the room.

It's just a sick joke, I think. *A terrible prank. It doesn't mean anything. Someone saw the interview and thought to have some fun at my expense.*

"That's it. That has to be it. Just someone stupid, just someone—"

And then I can't breathe as the truth dawns on me.

In the interview, and then article after article, so much came out about my time in the basement, so many details.

But not once did I ever . . . tell anyone . . . about the box of bees.

ACKNOWLEDGMENTS

There may be only one name on the cover of this book, but by rights, there should be many others. Books are a collaboration; don't let anyone tell you differently. To start, Liz Szabla, the best editor in the business. I'm so *freaking* lucky to work with her. As well as Rich Deas, who creates killer covers, book after book. And to the others at Macmillan Children's Publishing Group who work behind the scenes on my behalf, not to mention make me feel so welcome whenever I'm at an event or show up at the Flatiron: Jean Feiwel, Angus Killick, Nicole Banholzer, Mary Van Akin, Molly Brouillette, Lauren Burniac, Anna Roberto, Lucy Del Priore, Dave Barrett, Holly West, and Katie Fee, to name only a few. (There are many more! You know who you are.) I am beyond grateful to publish my books with them. Plus, I am over the moon that another novel is put to bed. Onward.

GOFISH

S. A. BODEEN

by V Imagery and Design

What did you want to be when you grew up?
An author, of course.

When did you realize you wanted to be a writer?
Grade five. Someone else won the creative writing award and it made me insanely jealous. (I did get the spelling prize, though.)

What's your first childhood memory?
When I was four, getting charged by Eleanor, one of our Holsteins. She had a calf and I got too close and I remember screaming and running for the porch. (I made it, obviously.)

What's your favorite childhood memory?
I grew up on a farm in a small town in Wisconsin. Every summer, my Aunt Connie and Uncle Bud and four cousins would come from Los Angeles. I thought they were like the Brady Bunch and they added color to my black-and-white life.

As a young person, who did you look up to most?
Captain Kirk. He always triumphed over the bad guy, was loyal to his friends, and protective of his crew. I watched *Star Trek* re-runs every day after school. You let someone into your living room five days a week and they tend to be fairly influential (as Oprah fans can attest).

What was your worst subject in school?
Art. I got a D+. No chance of me ever illustrating my own work.

What was your best subject in school?
Social studies. Although I couldn't take typing because world history was at the same time. Probably why I have a very un-orthodox way of typing . . .

What was your first job?
I always had to help around our farm, but my first paying job was picking strawberries the summer after sixth grade. Ten cents a quart. My take at the end of the summer was $34. I blew it all on a camera.

How did you celebrate publishing your first book?
It was ten years ago and my kids were little. I think we took them out to a McDonald's Playland or something.

What do you consider being a success in the field of publishing?
When your book is an answer on *Jeopardy!*

Where do you write your books?
Usually at the kitchen table.

Where do you find inspiration for your writing?
In things I read, see, watch. I'm also an eavesdropper out in public. Nosiness is good for inspiration, too.

Which of your characters is most like you?
I'm not sure I've written that one yet. But some days, I feel very akin to Eva in *Elizabeti's Doll*.

When you finish a book, who reads it first?
My critique group. I used to hand it off to family members, but that doesn't always work so well.

Are you a morning person or a night owl?
Definitely morning. I rarely stay up after 10 PM.

What's your idea of the best meal ever?
A pregame grill-marked bratwurst with sauerkraut at Lambeau Field.

Which do you like better: cats or dogs?
Cats, but dogs are a close second.

What do you value most in your friends?
Loyalty. Them liking me for who I am. And laughing at my jokes.

Where do you go for peace and quiet?
A hot shower that wastes much water. Or a movie by myself.

What makes you laugh out loud?
The Office. And Stephen Colbert.

What's your favorite song?
Toss-up between "Pride" by U2 and the "Moonlight" Sonata.

Who is your favorite fictional character?
Owen Meany. Harry Potter a close second.

What are you most afraid of?
Deep water. And tornadoes. Basically, Mother Nature in general.

What time of year do you like best?
Spring.

If you were stranded on a desert island, who would you want for company?
The Professor, so he could make me a laptop from a coconut.

If you could travel in time, where would you go?
To 1977, to see my seventh-grade self. I would tell her she will survive those years, and to soak up the drama and angst, because it will make for terrific story material one day.

What's the best advice you have ever received about writing?
It's easier to revise lousy writing than to revise a blank sheet of paper.

What do you want readers to remember about your books?
That they got them thinking.

What would you do if you ever stopped writing?
I'd be a spokesperson for Carmex, can't live without that stuff.

What do you like best about yourself?
I make a really good grilled-cheese.

SQUARE FISH

What is your worst habit?
Putting things off that I need to do.

What is your best habit?
I am a religious flosser.

**What do you consider to be your greatest
accomplishment?**
Actually finishing a novel. And maybe my master's degree.

SQUARE FISH

Six years ago, the outside world was destroyed. Eli's father built the Compound to keep them safe—that's how his family survived. But now, his father refuses to let them out, and Eli can't help but wonder if he'd rather take his chances outside. . . .

★ "A high-wire act of a first novel, a thriller that exerts an ever-tighter grip on readers."
—PUBLISHERS WEEKLY

COMPOUND

S.A. BODEEN

Eli's father built the Compound to keep their family safe. Now, they can't get out. He won't let them.

Read on for an excerpt!

PROLOGUE

T. S. ELIOT WAS WRONG. MY WORLD ENDED WITH A BANG the minute we entered the Compound and that silver door closed behind us.

The sound was brutal.

Final.

An echoing, resounding boom that slashed my nine-year-old heart in two. My fists beat on the door. I bawled. The screaming left me hoarse and my feet hurt.

Through my tears, the bear and elk on my father's shirt swam together. Beneath the chamois, Dad's chest heaved. The previous forty minutes had left us out of breath. Finally my gaze focused and went beyond him, searching. I gulped down a painful sob.

Had everyone made it?

Farther down the corridor I saw my weeping mother, dressed in a burgundy robe, dark tendrils dangling from her once-careful braid. Mom clutched my six-year-old sister,

Terese, a sobbing pigtailed lump in pink flowered flannel. From one small hand dangled her beloved Winnie the Pooh.

Behind them stomped my eleven-year-old sister, Lexie, dark hair mussed, arms crossed over the front of her blue silk pajamas. Not being brother-of-the-year material, I almost didn't care if she made it or not.

But my grandmother wasn't in sight.

"Where's Gram?" I shouted.

Dad patted my head, hard and steady, like I was a dog. He spoke slowly, in the same tone he used to explain to the household help the exact amount of starch he required in his shirts. "Eli, listen to me. There wasn't enough time. I waited as long as I could. It was imperative I get the rest of you to safety. We had to shut the door before it was too late."

The door. Always, the door.

Another look. No sign of my twin brother. He was the person I needed the most. Where was he?

My pounding heart suggested I already knew the answer. "Eddy?" His name caught in my throat, stuck tight by the panic rising up from my belly.

Dad whirled around, his tone accusing. "I thought Eddy was with you."

My head swung from side to side. Between sobs, the words barely eked out. "He went with Gram."

Dad's face clouded with indecision. Just for a moment. Had that moment lasted, it might have changed all of our futures. But Dad snapped back into control. "I still have one of you." With just six words, my childhood ended.

As did the rest of the world.

I knew what happened that night. We had been prepared. Other kids got bedtime stories about fairies and dogs. We fell asleep with visions of weapons of mass destruction dancing in our heads. Every evening, dinner included updates Dad downloaded from the Internet, updates on the U.S. involvement in the Middle East, the status of nuclear weapons programs in places like Iran and North Korea, names of countries that had been added to the list of those with WMDs.

Dad gripped my shoulders and pulled me away from the silver door, twisting me around to follow the rest of my family. What was left of it. I clung to my father's hand. He rushed ahead of me, his hand dropping mine.

I lifted my hand to my face and it reeked of fuel.

The corridor ended. We paraded through an archway strung with twinkling white lights, then entered an enormous circular room. The place reminded me of a yurt we'd built in school, only about eighty times bigger. The curved walls were made of log beams; the same type that crisscrossed over our heads in an intricate pattern. The roundness of the room was odd yet comforting.

Unlit logs sat in an elaborate stone fireplace, around which luxurious, overstuffed couches, love seats, and armchairs formed an audience. For a few seconds, despite the situation, my nine-year-old mind pondered what wonderful forts could be made with all those cushions.

Mom sat on a green couch and cradled Terese, while Lexie stood beside them, glowering. Dad lit kindling between the logs in the fireplace. The familiar smell of wood smoke wafted toward us, seeming out of place in a setting so distinctly unfamiliar. My father put his hand on my mother's shoulder. His knuckles were white. He chose that moment to tell my mother and sisters that Gram and Eddy hadn't made it.

The announcement made it real. Made it final. A verbal execution.

Wails erupted from inside me. Mom and Lexie cried, too.

I ran to my mother. She held me along with Terese. Lexie leaned against Dad, and his arms encircled her.

We stayed that way for a long time, my face crushed to Mom's bosom. She smelled of lilacs. As I sobbed, she stroked my hair. Like always, Mom's touch was comforting and warm. Even that night, that heinous night, her touch helped. Our cries sounded over the crackling of the logs. After a long while, sobs faded to sniffs and shudders, waning from fresh grief into leftovers.

Feeling the need to move, I stood up. I wiped my nose with my sleeve, and climbed onto a stool by a large bar with a stainless steel refrigerator behind it.

Dad flicked a switch.

A plasma television dropped down from the ceiling, blank monitor glowing. "I figured we'd be in here a lot." The blue from the television tinted Dad's face and blond hair in a garish way. He startled me when he threw his arms out to the side. "Cozy, yes? What do you think?"

"It's not what I expected." Mom's voice was shaky.

Dad rubbed his jaw. "What did you expect?"

I had a pretty good idea what Mom was thinking. In

third grade, I gave an oral report on nuclear war. If you lived in a target area like we did, you had approximately forty minutes after nuclear weapons were launched. Forty minutes to do what? Say good-bye to loved ones, stuff yourself with doughnuts, take a hundred-mile-an-hour joy ride: whatever one did with only forty minutes left to live.

If you were me, the son of Rex Yanakakis, billionaire? Those forty minutes were spent escaping to an underground shelter, built specifically for the Yanakakis family. Here, I would live out the next fifteen years in luxurious comfort while nearly everyone else perished. We hadn't seen the shelter, only heard Dad talk about it. So I think Mom felt like I did, a little surprised the place actually existed.

"I don't know." Mom's head swayed slightly. The movement caused a tear to drip off the slope of her nose. "At least it's quiet down here."

Dad observed her for a moment. Then he switched off the television. "Eli? Lexie? Want to see your rooms?"

Our grave circumstances had not yet sunk in. I was a robot, dazed, simply sliding off the stool to follow my father and my older sister. It felt like a dream. Through a doorway on the opposite side of the room from where we'd entered, we proceeded down a long carpeted hallway similar to the ones in our house in Seattle. Only difference was this one smelled of vanilla and had the constant hum of a generator.

Dad narrated as we walked. "All the walls are reinforced, as we discussed, to keep out radiation. But the concrete is not pleasant to look at, so all the rooms are finished in wallboard or wood. I didn't want you to feel surrounded by concrete and steel."

Dad stopped in front of a purple door. Lexie pushed it open and squealed. Leave it to her to cheer up over material possessions. Like something out of an Arabian Nights book, silk tapestries and curtains of bright colors were draped everywhere. A monstrous canopy bed ran the length of one whole wall. There was an exotic, cloying aroma. Incense maybe?

Lexie disappeared into the closet. When Dad talked about the Compound, he told us we'd have duplicates of everything we treasured. What an idiot I had been, to believe everything I cherished could be reproduced.

We left Lexie to explore and continued down the corridor. Dad indicated my room on the right. I pushed open the red door. Fresh smelling meadowy air blew softly into my face. A bed took up the entire near wall, but there was no canopy like Lexie's. Instead, I looked up at the night sky.

Dad's hand squeezed my shoulder. "The constellations rotate. It's timed to be accurate from sundown to sunup, and will alter with the seasons. You can even choose the southern hemisphere if you like. During the day the bulbs mimic the actual progression of the sun. Of course, you have artificial light available at any time, but I thought you might miss your sunsets."

My sunsets? Not just mine. I wanted to shout at him. They were Eddy's sunsets, too.

Every day since we were seven, Eddy and I sat on the front lawn of our estate and watched the sun set over Puget

Sound. The evening ritual began with Els, an old lady from Belgium, who was one of our family's cooks. Hardly taller than Eddy and me, she wore her silver hair in a bun and squeaked around in white orthopedic shoes. As a rule, she never smiled.

One evening after dinner, she set out ice cream and bowls for sundaes, then left us to make our own. Sometimes we'd make a little mess, usually just drippings on the counter, smears of chocolate sauce. But that day I dropped a scoop of ice cream on the red-tiled counter. Instead of just picking it up, I poured fudge sauce over it. Eddy giggled and squirted whipped cream on top. I added a few cherries. We laughed. Then we filled our dishes.

Before we were done, Els returned. She saw the chaos and must have known I had caused it. She shook her finger in my face, speaking in her strong accent: "Brat, you are always a brat." She grabbed me by one ear. Her pinching grip was extra firm. From decades of kneading, I imagined. She had no trouble dragging me out the door.

I fell to my knees on the soft lawn. My ear hurt and I rubbed it while scowling up at her. "I'm telling my dad!"

Els raised her hands. "What will he say? He tells you always, 'Go out, get fresh air.' I give you fresh air." She slammed the door.

Eddy had followed us outside with an ice cream sundae in each hand, splotches of whipped cream adorning his face. He sat down next to me and handed me a bowl. Banished to the lawn, we ate our ice cream and perceived the sunset as an actual event for the first time ever. The next day, we found ourselves waiting for it to happen again.

Sunsets, imitation or not, would no longer be the same.

Still, knowing my dad expected it of me, I lamely thanked him for the extravagant special effects. The room was done in the primary colors that appeal to boys of nine. One wall held shelves that stretched into the stars, and a speedy scan revealed my favorite books and other possessions. Copies, of course.

Dad asked me if I wanted to see more of the Compound.

I didn't. We would have to wait fifteen years, fifteen years before it would be safe to go outside. Which left more than enough time to see the rest of the Compound. Our new world. A new world I would soon hate.

Dad rubbed my shoulder. Suddenly his touch suffocated me. My stomach lurched, and I thought I might be sick. I wriggled down, away from his grip.

We went back to the family room. Terese slept on the couch. When Mom saw us, she shifted Terese off her lap and stood. Her eyes were vacant as she went behind the bar and made instant hot chocolate with marshmallows in the microwave.

I don't recall finishing my drink. I just remember feeling the emptiness in my gut. And the guilt. Nothing would ever be the same without Eddy, but I had to live with that. Why? Because it was my fault he wasn't there. My fault Eddy was dead. That night, I blamed myself.

Almost six years later, the feeling was just as strong. As was the feeling that all was not right in our new world.